CITY OF GLEAMERS

The Sheena Meyer Series
Book five

Books by L. B. Anne

Curly Girl Adventures Series:
Pickled Pudding
Zuri the Great
Tangled
Top Knot

Lolo And Winkle Series:
Go Viral
Zombie Apocalypse Club
Frenemies
Break London
Middle School Misfit
The Compete Collection

The Sheena Meyer Series:
The Girl Who Looked Beyond the Stars
The Girl Who Spoke to the Wind
The Girl Who Captured the Sun
The Girl Who Became A Warrior
City of Gleamers
Secret of Shadow and Light (Coming Soon)

Everfall Series:
Before I Let Go
If I fail

Brave New World:
Gemma Kaine: Sky Rider
Gemma Kaine: The Curse of Mantlay (Coming Soon)

Snicker's Wish, A Christmas Story

The Way to Storey

Five Things About Dragonflies (Coming Soon)

CITY OF GLEAMERS

The Sheena Meyer Series
Book Five

L. B. ANNE

JOA PRESS
FLORIDA

Copyright © 2021 L. B. ANNE
All Rights Reserved.

Cover Illustration by May Dawney
Pen and ink drawings by DM Baker
Edited by Michaela Bush
Proofread by Jessica Renwick

No part of this publication may be reproduced, stored in a retrieval system, or transmitted, in any form or by any means, electronic, mechanical, photocopying, recording, or otherwise without the written permission of the author.

This is a work of fiction. Names, characters, business, places, events, and incidents in this book are purely fictional and any resemblance to actual person, living or dead, is coincidental.

ISBN: 978-1-7362688-3-4

Unless otherwise indicated, scripture quotations are from the New King James Version ® Copyright © 1982 by Thomas Nelson, Inc. Used by permission. All rights reserved.

There is a gleam inside of all of us…

"…Not hoping to get to Heaven as a reward for your actions, but inevitably wanting to act in a certain way because a first faint gleam of Heaven is already inside you."
— C.S. Lewis

1

All girls have big ideas about the year they turn thirteen, I think. I know I did. That's because we become official teenagers. It's a big deal.

When I was ten years old, my Nana gave me a little pink journal with gold butterflies on the cover that she'd bought at a grocery store. One day, I stomped to my room, irritated about something, and wrote in it with a purple glitter gel pen:

Things are going to change big time when I turn thirteen!

Then, I made a list.

Kids other than Chana, Teddy, and Bradly would "get" me. A whole tribe of friends who were like me and shared my interests. You know, the crème de la crème kids. I'd get to wear my hair any way I wanted (I begged for faux locs.), watch PG-13 movies if I wanted, go to a Stevie Nicks concert, and drink Starbucks coffee—every flavor they had.

The last thing I expected to do at thirteen was—wait, I made a list (Yeah, I still do that.):
- ✓ see angels
- ✓ learn I'm a gleamer
- ✓ find out my best friend is a guardian angel
- ✓ fight a monster
- ✓ watch someone's father die
- ✓ become a warrior

I mean, I didn't even know Luke had a son until about an hour ago. That's how long I estimated it took us to haul ourselves out of that wicked house. Wicked as in evil, not crazy-good.

My heart no longer raced, but my brain felt energized. The neurons were firing like fireworks.

I wish I could tell you we were all fine after facing an evil force from a Netflix horror movie—that we walked to Justin's house, ate some of his infamous eggahamarye, and all went home like the same kids we awoke as that morning.

I wish I could say there was nothing else to worry about, and there'd be no more nightmares. But I couldn't. It was far from over.

I eyed our shadows just to the left of us, clumped together like a mountain with heads and feet. The wind whipped over my face, causing my eyes to tear, and washed away the eerie feeling from the basement that had draped over me and stuck there—right along with the musty basement odor.

Teila and Parker threw questions over my shoulder as the others listened intently. "How did you know? When did you know?" Blah, blah, blah...

Would Maleficent tell her kingdom everything she knew? No. She'd say something like, "Oh dear. Why on earth would I tell you? You should probably mind your business." And then turn them into frogs or something.

No, I couldn't tell them everything. Not about the angels and definitely not about the M-word.

"Was that it? That thing? Is it back? What was it called again?" asked Jasmine, one of the eighth-grade bookworms—the girls who always sat at their lunch table with their noses in books and rarely ate. I heard someone threw a wad of paper at Jasmine's head once, and she caught it without looking up from her book.

I bit my tongue, stopping the word from forming in my mouth, as if saying "the Murk" aloud might cause that dark-smokey-swirling-lava-flowing concoction of evil to appear. It was too soon after what we'd gone through.

"Look, I can't take any more questions right now, okay?" The words came out louder and harsher than I meant them to. But didn't they know my mind was just as blown as theirs? "BOOSH!"

"What was that?" asked Ariel.

"Oh, nothing. Just my brain exploding."

She looked at me oddly and giggled.

At least the questions stopped.

The thirteen of us walked slow and steady up the street. Close together. Everyone prepared to assist Chana if her legs gave out.

My thoughts went right back to the basement of that house. I was still kind of in shock about what had happened. Only minutes ago, I almost got sucked, along with Chana, into a glowing chest. What the heck was that, anyway? And Principal Vernon had been the one who'd held her captive down there.

My friends joined together to fight against something I couldn't begin to explain. How evil Principal Vernon must have been to contain the Murk inside him. And I couldn't see it when I touched him. How did he hide it?

I looked ahead at the corner, noticing how long it was taking to reach the end of the block. Was it possible we were walking forward but moving further away at the same time? No. That's not how things worked, and now wasn't the time to "let the crazy out," as my mom would say. If no one else mentioned it, I wasn't going to either.

My energized brain calmed down, and I was certain that if I stopped walking or sat for even a second, I'd fall asleep.

What they don't tell you about battle scenes in movies is that fighting for your life totally wears you out. Although, you don't notice it until afterward. It starts in your legs. An aching that tells you there's not much time before your limbs stop listening to your brain and you collapse.

Chana squeezed my hand, and I remembered what she'd said moments ago. "Some struggles are orchestrated to release your potential." Then she called me a warrior.

Sheena Meyer, mighty warrior. I chuckled inside. A thirteen-year-old wasn't exactly my idea of a warrior, but I certainly felt stronger. Not so much afterward, but during the battle.

Chana, wearing Corey's navy parka, looked like a child limping along in her father's coat. She pulled the hood tight around her neck over her wild ponytail and leaned toward me.

We walked like we'd just left the frontline of a war. Like in that movie about the Spartans. "You're not watching that," my dad had said. "You're too young."

But I did watch it—a little.

It's not my fault that it's hardwired into kids' brains from birth, to go against our parents' rules. They say, "Don't touch that, it's hot." What do you do? You touch it. Bam! You've got third-degree burns. "Don't ride your bike in the street." You do it anyway, hit a curb, fall off, and a dump truck drives over your bike. That kind of stuff. We can't help it.

Anyway, a kid like me knows people who know things. A boy from my after-school program hooked me up. He told me about a website where you can view bootleg films. So I went over to Chana's, and we watched the movie on her laptop. Her parents didn't police her internet usage like mine did.

That night, I learned parents sometimes know what they're talking about. Okay, maybe all the time.

"There's nothing new under the sun," my dad always says.

"We've been your age already. Anything you think of doing, we've done, so we know what's going on in that brain of yours," my mom always chimes in.

Look, nobody's perfect, so I'll admit I made a bad choice. That was one bloody flick, and the little I saw gave me nightmares about the parts I didn't even see. My overactive brain just created them.

But none of that compares to the real-life gleamer stuff I'm dealing with. My ten-year-old self would be shocked to find her life turned into a living PG-13 movie.

Except for us, Monroe Street was empty. And although I could feel my friends behind me and Chana and Ariel beside me, it almost felt like a dream.

We conquered that glob of evil as a team. We had faith. We had hope. And I led them. If I didn't have my left arm around Chana's back and my right hand holding her, helping her walk, I would've done a few fist pumps in the air.

I glanced around Chana and to the other side of me, examining everyone's faces. Some looked deep in thought, like Cameron. Parker looked relieved. Bradly watched

Bodhi. Ariel hummed happily to herself. Teddy watched me. He always did—making sure I was okay or checking if he could tell by my expression if I was hiding anything.

Corey walked at the rear of the group with his shoulders hunched and his hands in his pockets, shivering. He was ten times as brave as any of us. Justin was when he needed to be. And Teddy too, to protect me.

Are they all really okay? I wondered. I mean, after my first encounter with the Murk, was I? Or the second? Or the third? Or the—

"Uh, guys?" said Parker.

No one responded.

"Superhero squad?"

"Man, how many times do I have to tell you we're not superheroes? What's wrong now?" asked Cameron.

Parker pointed behind him. "Did anyone notice that guy following us?"

2

One by one, we stopped walking and looked behind us.

"What guy?" asked Corey.

Parker looked toward the houses to the right, and then to the left, confused. "He was right there."

"He probably lives around here. What did he look like?" asked Teddy.

"Taller than me. Corey's height. A teen, I guess."

"Was he cute?" asked Bradly.

"You have issues," Parker snapped.

Bodhi patted Parker's shoulder. "We've all got issues. But you're too paranoid, Bro. We all kinda are right now, so I get it. But you need to calm down. It's making you jumpy."

"I'm just saying, we need to pay attention to our surroundings," Parker mumbled. "Don't look at me when random-weird-guy leaps out of the bushes and grabs one of us."

"It's winter. There are no leaves or buds on anything. We can see right through the shrubs," said Teddy.

"Well, I'm just saying."

"Hold up, people," said Corey. "Look, man-boy. There's no one there." He grabbed Parker by the back of the neck and pushed him along. "Why do you have a beard coming in when you're only in eighth grade?"

Parker sucked his teeth.

"Can we get going? It's too cold for this," said Jasmine, pushing her scarf inside her coat. The day had started out especially warm. It was our first winter thaw, leaving ice dripping from the trees, roofs, and gutters of houses. Now, the temperature was beginning to drop again.

"Hey!" someone yelled.

"Sheesh, what is it going to take to get us off this creepy block?" said Teila.

Some of our classmates ran toward us from up the street. I didn't recognize who they were until they got closer.

"Look who decided to show up *after* the action," said Cameron. "Parker, now would be a good time to throw those poo bombs you had."

"Is that who you saw?" asked Jasmine.

"Nope," Parker replied.

They were more of the kids who remembered what happened on the field with the Murk, and they were all talking at the same time.

"Sorry, we're late."

"Did we miss it?"

"Where are you guys going?"

"Man, get out of here. I called you before I left," Cameron said to a boy named Tyler.

"We had to get rides and met up at the school like you said. But you were gone. Why didn't you wait for us? You guys look beat," Tyler replied. "What can we do?"

"It's been handled," said Corey.

"What happened to Chana? Are you okay?" asked a girl.

"I'm fine," she replied.

Tyler wiped his hand over the left side of his face. "Why are you staring? What's on me?"

"Nothing. Don't look away," I told him. He had two different eye colors, one brown and the other blue. The only part of his face not concealed by his hat and scarf.

"What's wrong?" asked Corey, stepping close to me.

Cameron stretched out his arm, placing his hand on Corey's chest to stop him. "Are they good?"

A tiny glint expanded and receded inside Tyler's pupil. They all had it, a touch of the gleam. "They're okay. One of us," I said, assuring Corey. "Unpuff your chest."

"Whatever that means—Whoa!" Tyler exclaimed while looking down at his Timberland boots. He lifted one foot an inch from the ground. "Does anybody else feel like they're standing on the counter next to the blender their mom just poured cubes of ice, bananas, oat milk, and protein powder into and turned on?"

"Wow, that detailed?" said Justin.

"You could've just said it felt like an earthquake or a tremor," said Teddy.

"Yeah, but I've never felt one of those. I felt my counter vibrate from the blender."

Jasmine ignored the conversation and turned to walk away. "Are we going?"

"Wait," I said, holding my hand up as I stared at the ground.

"I feel it too," said Ariel.

Everyone focused on the road.

I learned in science class that Michigan didn't normally have earthquakes. But if there was an earthquake in a neighboring state, we could sometimes feel it. Maybe there was a quake in Canada or Illinois.

Ripples formed in a puddle at the curb. With each pound of my heart, another formed. I looked up, wishing something as simple as a blender was vibrating the surface. But it wasn't a blender or an earthquake.

Something was coming.

3

A few of the kids who'd just joined us looked panicked. It was understandable. They'd seen what happened in the field behind Nana's house, and as far as they knew, the Murk was destroyed. Now, this.

"Don't worry," I told them.

What a lie. There was no telling what we were about to face—and within less than a half-hour of the last battle.

Suddenly, my legs didn't feel so weary anymore, and those neurons were starting to pop again like popcorn kernels frying in oil on a hot skillet. Slow, and then fast. *Pop. Pop. Pop-Pop-Pop!*

Logan moved closer to me. "Round two."

"What do you mean?" I asked, but I knew. *Don't say it. Don't say it. Don't say it*, I begged inside.

"I think it's back."

"What's back?" asked Tyler.

"Believe me, you don't want to know," Parker replied while looking around us.

The new kids stepped closer, touching even, as we prepared to face whatever was coming.

"Remember that time in the shed behind Sheena's house?" Bradly asked Cameron.

Cameron stared at her and then patted Teddy's arm fast and hard. "Yo, you remember that?"

"How could I not?" Teddy replied and looked at me with raised brows. I know he wasn't suggesting I may have forgotten our shed and former clubhouse lifted from the ground and slammed down with us inside it.

A hammering sound, resembling the pounding of a bass drum, repeated. It combined with the sound of metal hitting metal.

BOOM-CLANG! it went, but the beat was eerily off.

"Should we run? We should run, right?" one of the new kids nervously asked.

"This doesn't feel right. I think we should hide. We're standing in the street, out in the open," said a girl with two long blue-black ponytails, wearing glasses and a green wool cap.

"You can't hide from what can see you in the dark," said Ariel.

"Well, all-righty," the girl mumbled.

Ariel always surprised me with her random bouts of wisdom. Everyone else found her odd. She didn't say anything further or glance my way. Her attention was on the sky.

"Wait," said Tyler with a grin. He clapped twice and pointed at me. "You've got angels. Are they coming?" He looked up as though they'd appear.

"Yeah, where are they?" asked another boy.

I side-eyed him. *If I hadn't prayed for their eyes to be opened, to see what I saw on the field that night, I wouldn't have to hear this right now.*

"Fear is what it wants," said Logan.

I let go of Chana. "He's right. Our fear fuels it. Bodhi, come here."

He stepped forward.

"Keep her at the center of us. Everyone else, surround her," I instructed.

"Why?" asked Tyler.

"Late people don't ask questions," said Cameron. "Just do it."

The Murk had used Principal Vernon to try to take—what *was* it trying to take from Chana? Her angelical essence or power? Whatever it wanted, I wasn't going to let it happen again. It was my turn to protect her like she'd protected me since birth.

Chana half-smirked as if she knew my thoughts, and I could almost hear her in my head teasing me, calling me a warrior.

The instant I turned around, lightning streaked through large gray clouds high above the houses as they slowly glided together from opposite directions. When they collided, the flash was almost blinding. It illuminated the area around us with a brief spotlight.

"That's not possible. Clouds don't do that," said Bodhi.

"Do you hear that?" asked Teila.

It wasn't like the shrieking we heard in the shed that night, but close enough. It bellowed as the clouds concealed the sun. The wind picked up, and the hammering continued to attack our ears.

Everyone watched me.

"What is it?" asked Bradly.

"Who cares what it is? Why isn't anyone coming out of their houses or anything?" Tyler pulled down the scarf that covered his mouth. "No one is even looking out the windows to figure out what's happening. I know they can hear this, and their dishes are shaking out of their cabinets. Watch this. Help!" he screamed. "See? Nothing."

"Yo, calm down," said Corey.

At that moment, a siren blared.

"Someone's coming. Oh my gosh, thank you," said a girl.

An ambulance turned from the intersection and sped up the block. A police car followed with its lights flashing.

Tyler waved his arms wildly, and then let them drop to his sides as the patrol car passed by. "Did you see that? They drove right past us. How could they not see me waving like a maniac?"

Lightening cracked the sky in pulses like something was pounding on the other side trying to get out.

"Such a pity," I heard in a whisper.

"It's here," I said.

Logan's hand grasped mine for a moment. I looked into his eyes and nodded, and then looked at Ariel as she stared ahead, fixed and determined. "We're ready. Whatever comes, we're ready," I said, reassuring myself.

"No, we're not," yelled one of the new kids.

The sound grew unbearably loud, sending prickles up my spine.

"We're not afraid!" Corey yelled at the sky.

"Speak for yourself," said ponytail girl.

Something whipped around us, too fast to make out. A gray blur. We closed in tighter to each other.

My eyes were direct, ready for battle, stronger than I appeared. Even though I was only 5'2" and about one hundred pounds, in my mind, I was ten feet tall—just as big as my angel. Speaking of which, where was he—it? I had a damaged guardian angel, so shouldn't an archangel appear to fill in for her?

The roaring not only grew louder, but we could feel something nearing us. Some of the kids screamed.

"Hold it together!" said Cameron.

I peered ahead through the curls that blew over my eyes and didn't bother to push them back. *They're not ready for this. We need more gleamers like on the field that night*, was all I could think.

"Look at them," said a quiet voice inside me.

I glanced back at my friends. Logan, Cameron, Corey, Bodhi, Ariel, Teddy, Bradly, Justin, Jasmine, Parker, and Teila. Two others stood with them around Chana, facing outward around the circle. Not in fighting stances, but ready for whatever we had to do. The rest ducked. A few hugged each other as they waited.

A boy glanced at me and ran away from us.

"Wait for me," another yelled, following him.

One kid prayed aloud, really fast. "Lord, forgive me for everything I've ever done. And if you'll get me out of this,

I promise to never lie again, to obey my parents, to not get suspended anymore, and—and I'll give up *Fortnite*."

"Man, you must be crazy," Teddy mumbled.

The voice continued, "Those who stand are all you need."

Are you serious? Because... My heart beat loudly in my ears. Fast, and then so slow there was barely a beat. The faces watching me blurred.

I felt myself drifting away.

4

Everything went black for a moment.

"Sheena!" I heard from far away.

Chana's worried face came into view over me. "Sheena!"

"I'm okay," I said, looking up at her from the ground. "This is earth, right?"

Chana's brows rose. "What planet do you think you're on?"

"That was a joke."

"Not funny right now."

I thought it would ease their minds if I joked about it. They'd been watching me. I looked like I'd blacked out, but in that brief moment, I saw so much.

I had a sense of being released from my world, Monroe Street, Muskegon, Earth. Immediately, I was transported to a battle in the sky. Not exactly *our* sky, but not exactly space either. Stars twinkled in the distance. They were so much brighter than the ones I viewed from my bedroom window at night.

Angels were on one side of a divide. I'd never be able to put into words how spectacular they were. Their splendor left me in awe. My archangel, glowing and almost translucent, pointed, and I turned. On the other side of the divide, behind me, was something dark enough to blot out the stars. But as soon as I saw it, in a split second, I was back on Monroe Street.

"Seriously, I'm okay. I haven't eaten today," I lied.

Ariel came to my right side, and Justin the left. She looked into my eyes as she held my hand and arm and pulled. From her expression, I almost thought she knew the truth, but how could she?

"This isn't a good time to pass out, you know," said Bradly.

"Girl, I thought you were dead. I was about to be like, see ya, I'm out," said a boy.

Corey watched the sky and all around us as everyone else focused on me. "It's not over. Everyone needs to get back in place. Chana, stay in the center," he told her.

Cameron stood behind me and next to Teddy as the group formed a tight circle around Chana again instead of around me. "Are you ready, Angel Girl?" he asked.

I nodded, and we waited as the afternoon grew colder and the ground continued to shake. *If it's going to attack, what's it waiting on? Just do it already.* "Waiting increases fear," I replied to my thoughts. *The longer it takes, the louder it gets, the more the ground shakes. The more afraid we become.*

Bradly had just brought up our experience in the shed. She was absolutely right. This *was* like that time.

"It's not real," I said.

"What?" Bradly asked.

It was so obvious now. Like someone shaking your doorknob and controlling your lights from outside your bedroom to make you think a ghost is doing it. Plus, whenever the Murk appeared, there was a stifling heat that came with it. That didn't happen this time.

I stepped away from the group.

"Sheena, come back," said Teddy.

"It's not real. It's an illusion."

Teddy followed close behind me. "Get back here," he demanded, sounding like my father, as usual.

"What we're seeing isn't real," I repeated, turning to him. "Like a three-dimensional roaring lion."

"A hologram?"

"Yes. A roaring lion that will never bite, because…"

"It's not real," Teddy said, finishing the sentence. He turned back to our group. "It's not real."

"Say it. It's not real!" I yelled.

Ariel nodded and repeated after me. Then Cameron and Bradly said it too. Each person joined in until they all repeated it together, believing it.

Within seconds, the wind died down and the bellowing subsided.

"It's over, right?" asked one of the girls. Her eyes begged me to tell her what she wanted to hear.

We glanced at each other, none of us prepared to lie and tell her yes. It was never over with the Murk.

Just as I opened my mouth to try and say something reassuring, Mr. Tobias's house exploded.

5

The blast hurled us across the street. I smacked into the asphalt on my side, and for a split second thought my dad stood over me.

Through the smoke I saw my friends on the ground, shielding their heads as pieces of wood and debris tore through the air and landed around us.

Pain shot through my shoulder. Too dazed to move, I grimaced as I watched what was left of the burning home. Somewhere close, Ariel coughed. Someone moaned. Cameron scrambled over, hitting at the flames on Bodhi's leg.

Chana rolled onto her stomach, watching me.

Hands pulled at my coat and lifted me up. I looked up at Corey and the bloody scrapes on his hands. "We've gotta get out of here," he said. "The police are coming."

"Help them up," he instructed someone.

"Teddy! Where's Teddy?" I screamed.

"I'm here!" he groaned. Through the smoke I could see Logan helping him up.

We all stood and faced Mr. Tobias's property.

"I can't believe it's gone," I said to myself.

"That was—*HUFF*—wild—*HUFF*," Tyler said, breathing as if he'd just run a marathon.

"Where's your inhaler?" asked Bodhi, while pulling at his pant leg. There was a hole in his jeans, but the flames hadn't burned through his layers.

Tyler held up a finger, pulled his asthma inhaler from his coat pocket, shook it, inhaled deeply, and exhaled. He brought the inhaler to his mouth and inhaled as he pushed it down.

We waited as he repeated it.

"I'm good. Thanks for asking," he said sarcastically.

"Okay, I don't know about anybody else, but I'm getting out of here. Plus, people are starting to wonder what we're doing, I think," said Teila, pointing to a woman holding her door open and looking over at us. Other doors were opening, and people were coming out into their yards.

"*Now* they wanna come outside?" asked Parker.

"You guys need to get going," I told the new kids. "Can you make it?"

"I think so. Everyone's a little shaken up, but no one's hurt. Are you sure?" asked Tyler.

"Yeah, go." I could already hear the horn beeping and the whirr of a fire truck's siren.

"Well, you don't have to tell me twice," said one of the girls.

"It sure didn't take much convincing," said Cameron.

Corey shook his fist. "You can leave, but anyone who opens their mouth about any of this will meet these—"

Teddy grabbed Corey's fist and pushed it down.

"We won't, we won't," said Tyler. "I don't even want to remember it. Let alone figure out why none of us were hurt."

I held onto Chana again, although I didn't think she needed assistance any longer. We all walked hurriedly now. Even if that hammering and screeching and what we saw was just an illusion, Mr. Tobias's house exploding was not. Someone or something was watching us.

A patrol car siren blared as we turned the corner. The police would be there any minute.

"We should run," said Corey. "Can you run, Chana?"

She shook her head.

"But we didn't do anything," said Jasmine.

Justin pushed her along. "But we look like it. Corey's right. Someone called the police, and I'm not trying to have a record. Remember, some of us were screaming. Then a house explodes? Nope, we need to get out of here."

"There's no time. Those sirens are close. We need a miracle," said Teddy.

"Hide!" yelled Parker.

We tried to determine which way to go and only bumped into each other.

Tires squealed as a UPS van pulled to a stop beside us. "Get in!"

We stood there, looking at the driver.

I couldn't move. I stared at his caramel skin and short curly hair.

"What are you waiting for?" he asked.

Corey pushed us. "Go!"

The back door of the van slid up, and we crowded in all the way to a dolly near the back wall and pressed together in the center between the racks of boxes. As soon as we were all inside, the driver told us to hold on and closed the back door.

We waited, barely breathing as what sounded like fire trucks, an ambulance, and police cars sped by.

The driver started the engine and pulled away from the curb.

"Who is this guy?" asked Cameron.

The door on the wall next to the driver's seat slid open. "You okay back there, Sheena?" he yelled behind him.

"You know him?" Chana asked.

"Ye-yes," I replied, still in shock.

"Who is that?" asked Teddy.

"You asked for a miracle, didn't you?" I held my hand out, palm up toward the driver. "Miracle."

"I don't care who he is. He came through for us," said Corey.

"Where is Logan?" I asked abruptly, trying to see around everyone.

"I thought he got in," said Teddy.

"Did we leave him?"

"No, I looked. No one was behind me. I was the last one in," said Corey.

"This day has been way too crazy," said Teila.

I nodded. "Welcome to my new normal."

"Sir, where are we going?" asked Bodhi.

"Away from whatever was going on back there. Where would you like to be dropped off?"

"Yo, dude is cool," said Corey.

"We were going to my house, right around the corner from where we were," said Justin.

"No problem. I'll circle back."

Everyone can see and hear him, I thought.

"I'm just glad to be off that street," said Teila.

We could feel the van turning corners, twisting, and weaving through streets, taking us back through the neighborhood.

"Is everyone still coming to my house or what?" asked Justin.

"You don't want to be alone, huh?" Parker pushed him, but he didn't budge. "Move over, you're squashing me."

"Look, everybody's squashing everybody."

"A house just blew up," Bradly said. Everyone watched her. "A house just blew up," she repeated, barely above a whisper. "Someone could've been in there," she continued. "Like that homeless guy we found. *We* could've been in there. I want my mom."

"Bradly...," said Cameron.

"I want my mom," she screamed.

Teila put her arm around her. "Calm down. It's okay. The house was empty. It had to be." But she didn't sound so sure.

"I want to go home," said Jasmine.

"No one is going home. At least not yet. We need to talk about everything that happened. Don't tell me all of you don't have fifty million questions like I do," Cameron whispered.

"Questions for who?" I asked.

"You," Parker, Teila, and Justin said in unison.

"I'm on Hudson Street," Justin yelled to the driver. "The beige house near the end of the block. The one with the big pine tree."

The driver nodded. "I'll let you guys out right here at the corner."

We all exited the van through the door at the front and hopped off the step onto the street. But I stepped back inside. "What are you doing here?" I whispered. "You're supposed to be a nurse, not a UPS driver."

"I am whatever I choose to be." He lowered his head, as if I should understand.

"Sheena," Teddy called.

"Thank you, nurse—I mean, Javan."

Instead of a goodbye, he gave me that kind grin he always had. I backed out of the truck and watched as it pulled off, expecting it to disappear into thin air.

"May your vision be true," I heard in a whisper.

My eyes widened.

"What's wrong, Sheena?" asked Ariel.

"Nothing," I said as I tried to shake off an eerie feeling.

That was him. The archangel. He showed himself. What does that mean? Something felt very wrong.

I looked at Chana for answers, but she avoided my gaze. She hadn't said a word while we were in the van.

"Look!" Ariel said, pointing at Logan as he walked up to us.

"Logan!" I cried. "Where did you go?"

He shrugged. "I stayed behind to see what was going to happen."

"What *did* happen?" asked Teddy.

"They won't let cars on the street. They evacuated the other houses too."

Teddy scratched his head. "Did they go inside—"

"No. I was hoping they would, but someone told an officer it was empty."

I cleared my throat. "We're all going to Justin's house."

"I know."

"You do?"

"That was the original plan," said Logan.

"So you waited for us?" I whispered as we followed Justin. "But that would mean you knew we were coming back here. Which doesn't make sense because he could've dropped us all off at home."

"Shh…" Logan stopped and faced the opposite direction.

I stopped beside him. Flurries landed atop his dark curls and on his eyelashes.

I tilted my head. "What's up? Why'd you stop?"

He stared down the sidewalk. I looked too but saw nothing. "Is it back?"

"What's up with him?" yelled Corey as he ran back to us and stood there like he was Superman or something, looking around.

"Come on, Logan. Let's get going, huh?" I said with a nudge.

I didn't understand Logan's expression. He wanted to tell me something, I was sure. For a moment I thought he was going to run. Instead, he turned and followed me.

We walked to the front of the group.

"You saw him too, didn't you?" Parker asked Logan.

"Let it go, man," said Bodhi.

6

With each step, Chana became her old self. Her body straightened and strengthened, and her limp decreased until she pushed away anyone who tried to help her.

Justin opened the chain link gate to his yard, and we followed him up the stairs of the porch.

"Ma! Ma, I'm home!" he called through the house after unlocking the storm door and the shockingly yellow front door. "Come in, guys."

The twelve of us squeezed into the narrow foyer, unsure about going too far inside but happy to no longer be outside with whatever watched us.

It's funny how you can feel safer when parents are home. They don't even have to be your own.

The decor in Justin's house reminded me a lot of Mr. Tobias's—old-fashioned. But this room was filled with a hodgepodge of pieces. A French vintage sofa, a velvet recliner, a modern coffee table, and paneling on the walls.

And it smelled of cinnamon and bacon rather than ointment. I immediately felt at home, like I was at Nana's house.

There were pictures of Justin everywhere, from him as a baby crawling, to him a foot taller than all the other kids playing flag football, to him now in middle school.

"That you, J? You back?" a woman's voice called out. "Whew-we! Did you hear that explosion? Shook the whole house."

"Yes, Ma'am!" he replied and held up his pointer finger. "Hold up a minute," he said, and then disappeared through a door at the far end of the room.

We listened to the murmur of their voices as we looked around.

Teddy whispered something to Cameron.

"Let's go see," he replied, and they walked off through a doorway at the back of the room.

"Where are they going?" asked Ariel.

I shrugged. "I don't know."

"Is anyone else sore?" asked Bodhi.

I was beginning to feel it too, as well as a few bruises and scrapes.

Ariel placed her hand on my shoulder, and I saw it. I mean for the first time ever, I saw energy release from her hand and flow into my shoulder. My gleamer abilities were kicking in. The pain left me, and I instantly felt lighter and in a better mood.

"Better?" asked Ariel.

"Yes."

Unexpectedly, she reached for Logan. He moved aside. "I'm okay," he said. *Does he know she's a healer gleamer?*

"Sorry," said Ariel, looking away. She glanced at Logan again, and he returned her gaze.

Cameron and Teddy ran back into the room.

"Where did you go?" I asked.

"To see if we could see anything out the back window," Cameron replied.

Parker sat at the piano bench next to the entrance into a hallway and lifted his hand to tap a key.

"Don't," said Teddy.

Atop the piano were music books, a hands-praying figurine, trophies, and more photos.

Justin hurried back into the room, rubbing his hands together. "All right, let's eat."

"I can't believe you can even think about food right now," said Teila. "I feel kind of—"

"Horrified, petrified, frightened, freaked out?" asked Parker.

"Stop it," said Cameron. "Justin said, 'let's eat,' so let's eat." He walked ahead of us into the hallway. But his undaunted persona didn't fool me. He was as bothered as everyone else about what happened.

Corey walked ahead of me and brushed against a picture on the wall. I straightened it. It was old, vintage-looking. Muskegon from years ago. I recognized the Hackley Public Library and could just make out tiny dark writing beneath a smudge at the bottom. I wondered what the faded markings were below the buildings.

Justin led us down the short hall and into a yellow kitchen painted as bright as the front door. Someone's favorite color, I figured. I kept looking back at the wall. That picture was somehow familiar.

"Don't you have to ask first?" Teddy was saying as I walked in. "Or maybe you just did."

"Nope." Justin shook his head.

"You said, 'Ma'. I thought you lived with your grandmother," said Bodhi.

"I do. My grandma raised me. I took the grand part off and just call her Ma."

"Where's the bathroom?" asked Parker.

Justin pointed to another hallway. "First door on the left."

Parker nodded and left the room.

'Ma,' as Justin called her, walked in wearing a worn, fuzzy bathrobe. She stopped cold in front of us with wide eyes. Her hand flew to the stocking cap that covered her head. "Why on earth didn't you tell me there were people here?"

"Ma, I just did."

"You didn't tell me they were inside the house! I don't have my wig on!"

From the way she talked, I didn't think she had her teeth in either.

She looked around for something, so I handed her a wooden spoon. That's what my Nana would've wanted.

"Ma!" Justin yelled as she chased him. Well, not really chased. She kind of shuffled along. She was so small, and he was so big. It was like watching a puppy chase a horse.

We backed out of the way. All but Logan. He kept looking out the window that faced the backyard.

"Whew!" She placed her hands on her hips and breathed deeply. "I'm sorry you had to witness this foolishness. Justin didn't introduce us."

Justin frowned. "That's because you didn't give me a chance to. You just went to swatting."

"You kids can call me Ma." Her expression was of pure warmth, even if she was irritated with Justin.

"Hi, Ma," we all responded.

Ariel stepped forward. "I'm—"

Ma waved a hand at her. "Too many names. Don't even try to tell me. I'll only forget. I don't think I've ever had so many childrens in my house at one time."

Childrens?

"Justin said he would make us some eggahamarye," Cameron said and hugged her.

"Cameron, you here too?" she gushed.

I realized glasses were another thing she would've put on had she known we were in the house.

She placed a hand on her hip and turned to Justin. "Beanie, did you tell them you were going to cook in my kitchen?"

Chuckles came from Corey, Bodhi, and Teddy. "Beanie?"

"Yes, Ma'am," said Justin.

"Then get to it, because I'm not cooking. I'm watching my shopping channel, and Gloria is about to bring out some new kitchenware."

For a moment, I envied her. Living her life knowing nothing of the evil forces haunting kids. She didn't have to deal with angels or exploding houses. Her life was as simple as watching a shopping channel.

"Are you sure?" asked Justin. "Are you done embarrassing me now?" he said as she walked away. "Why are you guys standing there? You're inside. Take your coats off.

"Corey," Justin said and held up a teabag.

Corey nodded.

Bradly pointed at a door that was cracked open. "Can I close that?"

"It's just a closet," Justin said as he took a carton of eggs from a shelf in the refrigerator and placed it on the counter along with a plastic container.

He'd acted like it was no big deal, but he stopped what he was doing and watched along with the rest of us as Bradly walked over to the door. She looked inside the closet and closed it. "It makes me feel better. It felt sort of creepy."

"Now you sound like me," said Parker.

"All right," said Teila, hopping up from her seat at the table. "I have to do something to take my mind off everything. Let us help you. One of us can scramble the eggs, one of us shreds the cheese—"

"Cracking eggs is not as easy as it looks. Ask my kitchen floor," Parker said with a huff.

"There's no cheese in this dish," said Justin.

"Trust me, you'll like it. It'll take it up a notch. Eggahamarye 2.0. And I saw some cheese in there when you opened the refrigerator, so don't say you don't have any."

"Sounds good to me," said Teddy.

"Yeah, Beanie," Cameron joked. "Big ole butter bean."

"I don't eat cheese," said Bodhi.

Bradly stood beside him with her elbows on the counter, wrapping her waist-length braids around her neck. "Yeah, we don't eat cheese."

Justin grabbed a cast-iron skillet from the oven. "Half with cheese. Half without. And Cameron, since you've got jokes, you're reheating the ground beef." He slid the container over to him. "This was left over from spaghetti night."

Cameron opened the lid. "Sheesh, how much spaghetti does it take to feed you? There's still enough ground beef for about ten people!"

"We make extra for taco night."

"Makes sense," said Bodhi.

"Still, there's only two of you." Cameron shook his head.

The teapot whistled, and Corey squeezed around them, grabbing a cup from the coffee mug tree.

"Let's see... Eggahamarye. Eggs, hamburger meat... What's missing? Oh, what about the rice?" asked Teddy.

Justin searched the refrigerator and opened and slammed shut the brown cabinets beside it. "Aww man, we're out. How about cauliflower rice? There's a bag in there on the bottom shelf."

Teddy tossed Corey a green and white bag from the freezer, and they made faces like something stunk. "This better be good."

"You won't even notice it's not rice," said Justin.

Corey scrunched his nose. "I bet we will."

"Are you hungry?" Ariel asked.

"Not really," I said, but my belly betrayed me and growled loudly.

"Was that you?" asked Teddy.

"Shut it."

"Let's have toast too," said Parker.

Justin held a loaf of bread like a football and tossed it to him. "Get to toasting. The toaster is right in there," he said, pointing at the pantry closet.

"You have peppers and onions?" asked Bradly.

"Wait a minute. You guys are messing up my recipe," Justin said. "Plus, that's too much work. This is supposed to be quick eats."

Corey slipped between them. "Step back. I've got it," He set his furry hat on a chair and washed his hands at the kitchen sink with dish detergent. It left a lemony scent in the air, and I noticed it didn't sting his cuts. How was that possible?

I glanced at Ariel, and she grinned. "Oh."

Corey was pretty handy in the kitchen, but then again, when was he not?

I kept one eye on Chana and the other on Logan while thinking about the last time I saw nurse Javan. He had let me in the NICU at the hospital. I had prayed for the babies and when I opened my eyes, I saw the guardians over each child. *But why did he appear today, and to all of us, and after everything?*

"Bradly, what are you doing?" asked Teddy, interrupting my thoughts.

"We're live," she replied, turning her phone toward him. "Don't just stand there with your mouth open, say hello to everyone."

"Oh, no you didn't," said Cameron.

"Are you kidding me?" asked Parker.

Bradly turned her phone to him. "Nope."

Cameron crept up behind her and snatched the phone from her hands.

"Hey!" She exclaimed as she reached around him, trying to take it back.

He held it above his head. "Can you keep it down? Look at us. Don't we look like we've been flung through the air from the force of an explosion?"

Bradly's face fell. "Oops."

"Oops, she says."

Logan had been leaning against the wall, silently watching it all. He walked toward them, grabbed the hair at the top of his head, and released it. "Umm... I hate to interrupt your whole cooking reality show you've got going on, but have all of you forgotten we left a body in that house?"

"We're trying to forget," said Parker.

Corey punched him on the arm.

"Ow!"

"That's his father," Corey said in a hushed tone. "Could you be a little sensitive?"

Everyone looked at Logan as if just realizing Luke was his father.

"I think I know how we can tell the police he's there, but still keep us out of it," I told them.

"I need to eat something," said Chana, sounding like she was back to her old self, but tired.

"Let's hurry and get this done. Give Chana these saltine crackers for now," Justin said, tossing the box across the counter. "Do you want some cheese to spray on it?"

"Cheese from a can? Are you kidding me?" asked Parker. That was quickly becoming his go-to phrase.

"Gross," Chana said and shook her head.

Justin kicked the refrigerator door shut with his foot. "More for me."

Everyone except for me, Chana, and Logan, gathered around watching the cooks. Chana sat at the table, eating her crackers and staring at the clock on the wall. "It's the ninth hour," she mumbled and closed her eyes.

Before I could ask what she meant, Ariel leaned over Chana's chair and wrapped her arm around her shoulders. "We should call your parents now. I hope I'll be there when they see you. They're going to be so happy and crying and—"

"Please stop," Chana mumbled.

"But—"

"Water."

"Huh?" Ariel asked.

Chana gestured at the crackers on the table. "Can you get me some water before these crackers cut off my air supply?"

Ariel hopped away, and Chana closed her eyes again. I guess she could feel me watching her, because without opening her eyes, she said, "Check on him."

"Him" could only mean Logan. What, maybe an hour ago, he'd pretty much overloaded Luke with some kind of energy to save me. Who does that? Who kills their own father? But what I really wanted to know was *why* he would do that.

He faced the back window with his head low. The more I watched him, the more the feeling grew that something was very wrong. But I wasn't sure if it had to do with him or the Mu—M-word.

I stood, rubbing my hands together, and walked over to him. "You know, they're all preoccupying themselves with cooking to hide how they're really feeling about everything that happened today. Don't you think?"

Logan didn't respond.

I cleared my throat. "I—uh... I'm sorry we're so insensitive. I can't imagine how you must feel right now. I mean, about your father. Are you okay?"

"Are you?" he replied.

"Yeah, I just—"

"You're not acting like the Angelus Bellator."

"I heard you say that to Luke. What does that mean?"

"You need to focus."

"Is that the translation?"

"No." He shook his head and pointed at the backyard.

I looked out at the snow-covered lawn and the fence beyond it. There were holes in the snow from where little feet had run through the yard. A rabbit or squirrel, or maybe a cat. And debris from the explosion lay everywhere. Through the bare shrubs and chain link fence, I could see fire trucks on Monroe Street. Justin's backyard faced Mr. Tobias's backyard with an alley between them.

"I don't see anything."

"Keep watching," he said.

I'm watching, I sang in my head. It felt just like one of those Mr. Tobias-teaching-moments. I imagined him now, saying, "You're blocking yourself—limiting your vision. There is a deeper reality than what is. Close your eyes and concentrate. Open your eyes with an awareness of what is really happening around you."

I closed my eyes and blocked out my friend's voices, the sizzle of the frying pan, and the water running from the kitchen faucet. When I reopened them, I didn't jump or gasp.

"What in the entire universe is that?"

7

I stepped closer to the window, watching a translucent metallic shimmer fade in and out above the ground at the center of the yard. It was about four feet in height and a foot wide. It glimmered mostly gold, but with hints of pale pink and jade green.

It was beautiful, strange, and eerie at the same time.

"What are you guys talking about over here?" Teddy came up behind us and grabbed both of our shoulders, looking out the window.

The shimmer disappeared.

I swallowed hard. "Nothing. Uh…" It took a moment for me to turn away from the window. "We need to make an anonymous call to the police; I was going to tell you that a moment ago."

"About Luke," Logan added.

Teddy's brows rose. "And say what?"

I held my hand out toward the window, pointing toward Mr. Tobias's backyard. "That somebody saw the guy on the news reports going into that house next door."

"How can we do that without the call leading back to us?" asked Bodhi.

"That's easy," said Corey.

"How?"

"I'll tell you when I'm done." He scraped the peppers off the chopping board and into a skillet.

A few minutes later, Justin announced, "Din-din is served! I'm coming in hot!" He set the pans of eggahamarye on the cast iron trivets on the counter.

"That is not what that phrase means," Cameron said, shaking his head.

"I don't think I can watch," I said, covering one eye and squinting with the other. But I couldn't turn away either.

"This is really happening," said Teddy.

Justin filled not a plate, but a platter with his infamous eggahamarye. Then he squirted ketchup over the entire thing and looked around at all of us, who stood with our mouths open.

"What? It's not complete without ketchup."

"Ketchup is one thing, but did you leave any for the rest of us?" asked Cameron.

I didn't eat anything. The eggahamarye looked appetizing enough, but I couldn't. My stomach tightened into knots. I was bothered by everything that had happened and whatever that was outside. I glanced at Chana, and she made a face at me. We needed to figure out how to explain where she'd been and how we found her.

"No worries," she said, as if reading my mind.

When everyone was done eating, we cleared the dishes. "Hey, we're out," said Cameron.

Justin followed us. "Are you guys seriously leaving?"

"Yeah, I need to get home now, Bubble Belly. Or should I say, Beanie," said Chana, sounding like her old self.

"Hey, hey, stop calling me that, and get your hand off my bubble—I mean stomach. At least I wasn't the one thinking I had wings. 'It tried to take my wings,'" he mimicked her.

"All righty," I said, changing the subject. "We need to get going."

"Wait," said Justin. He hurried away and came back with a jacket. "Here." He handed it to Corey. "You're the only one big enough to fit it, and Chana is still going to need your coat."

"Good looking out," said Corey. He held his fist upright for a bump on top, then put on the jacket.

We all walked out onto the porch.

"Should we say goodbye to his grandmother?" asked Ariel.

"No, she's good," said Justin. "I'm the one you should be worried about. I don't think I want to be alone. Does anyone want to stay over?"

"You are too big to be so afraid," said Corey.

"I'm not. I'm thinking about when it gets dark. My mind is going to remember everything in vivid detail. Not only that, look where I live. I'm behind those two horror houses—I mean, horror house," he said pointing toward Mr. Tobias's land and the house beside it where Luke's body lay.

"You'll be okay. You've got your grandmother with you," said Bodhi.

"Are you serious?" He lowered his voice as if he were telling a scary story around a campfire. "Picture her in the dark with the wrinkles and a flashlight under her chin." He shivered.

"Stop thinking about that kind of stuff," said Cameron.

Parker's voice trembled. "Yeah, you're scaring the girls."

"That *is* pretty creepy, though," said Teddy, trying to hide his amusement.

Justin rubbed his eyes. "Plus, some things from today you can't unsee."

He was right about that.

"I know what you guys need right now," said Chana. "Go ahead, Sheena. Give him some of your warrior-leader wisdom."

Yeah, she was definitely back to her old self.

Everyone waited, expecting me to make some grand announcement.

"Well, you could…" I wracked my brain for something wise to say. "Just—I've got nothing."

"Pray," said Cameron.

I should've thought of that.

"Before you go to bed," he added.

"Me?" said Justin.

"Why not you?" asked Corey.

Cameron nodded. "Trust me. It helps."

"You're a pastor's son. I expect that from you," Justin replied.

"Try it," Cameron urged him.

"And say what?" Justin yelled as we walked away. "Sure, just leave me here with a woman wearing a stocking cap, looking like Gollum."

"Justin, are you out there talking about me?" his grandmother yelled.

I guess a hearing aid was the one thing she didn't need.

"No, ma'am," he lied.

The door opened, and Ma hobbled outside and onto the porch, wearing a turban style head wrap this time, swatting at him. "Beanie, get yourself inside this house."

"Bye, Ma," we said, and laughed as she shut the door. We could still hear her fussing at him as we turned up the street.

The smell of smoke was still strong in the air. It was hard not to look in the direction of Monroe Street as we crossed the intersection.

Logan pulled my arm, slowing me down, so everyone else was ahead of us. Teddy slowed also, watching.

"Look behind us," he whispered.

8

It was beautiful. Iridescent. Shimmering in and out of focus. The kind of thing that made you want to step closer to get a better look, and perhaps touch it, regardless of your mind shouting, "Don't do it!"

"Is it an angel?" I asked.

Logan didn't respond, and I wondered if he knew his silence was unnerving at times.

"What are you guys looking at?" asked Teddy.

"Nothing. I thought I saw something," I responded, ignoring his gaze. Where I was concerned, Teddy didn't know what it meant to mind his business. I wanted to punch him for always trying to figure me out or asking questions.

Chana walked between Ariel and Bradly and glanced back at us. I took it as a cue for me to get up there with them.

Corey hurried up the walk, and I fell in step with him and Cameron. Everyone else picked up their pace to catch up. He led us to a store a few blocks up. A brick building that took up most of the corner. The windows above our heads were covered in beer and soda posters, but you could see inside through the doors.

"Watch a pro work," Corey said.

"What are you going to do?" asked Teddy.

Cameron pulled his cap down. "Whatever you're going to do, hurry. It's getting colder out here. Too cold to be walking."

Corey whispered something to Cameron, and he grinned. "Let's do it."

"Well, we're not waiting out here," said Bradly.

Corey shrugged. "Fine, but don't interfere."

A bell dinged as we pushed the door open. Only a couple of us walked in at a time, so it didn't appear we were together.

A man stood at the counter in front of the candy bars and next to the machine warming the taquitos and potato balls. He placed a toothpick in the corner of his mouth and pulled wrinkled lottery tickets from the pocket of his duckshell work jacket and studied them.

"Give me two more," he told the cashier and set the money on the counter.

The cashier sounded half asleep. "That'll be four dollars."

The man tapped the money.

Corey stood behind him as if he were waiting in line. "Excuse me, sir."

The man ignored him, so he spoke louder. "Excuse me, sir! May I use your phone to call my father? My phone is dead."

I pretended to study the assorted brands of bubble gum on the rack beside them. Ariel picked one up and tried to hand it to Chana. She waved it away.

"You got any black licorice?" I asked the cashier. He pointed at the candy, and Chana's eyes lit up.

The man studied Corey for a moment.

"A girl should've done it," said Teddy.

To our surprise, the man handed Corey his phone. "Stay right there and call 'em."

"No problem," said Corey. He pretended to tap several digits, but really only pushed three. Then he turned his back.

"So what scratch-offs do you like the best?" Cameron asked loudly. "I bet you've won a ton of money."

"Oh, I get it. He's distracting him." I whispered to Chana.

"Someone gave me some for Christmas once," Parker said. He wasn't even supposed to be helping.

"Someone get him," I whispered.

"I won five dollars," Parker told the man. He lifted his hand for a high-five. The man stared at it as if he had cooties.

"Ah, yeah, Dad. Okay. Bye," Corey said loudly. "Thank you for trusting me with your phone," he told the man as he handed the phone back to him.

The guy grunted rather than responding.

"May the Lord shine on you and be gracious to you. You shouldn't gamble, though," Corey said, and then he walked out the door.

"Sheesh, you can't use the guy's phone and then tell him what to do," said Teddy.

"I need an energy drink," said Bradly.

"Your mom lets you drink those?" I asked.

"What does an energy drink have to do with parents? They don't card you for it."

"Okay, go and get your can of carbonated caffeine then."

"I will," Bradly said with a flip of her braids. She walked away and came back with the can.

Before she could put it on the counter, Bodhi snatched it from her. "Don't you dare," he said and took the can back to the shelf.

Bradly grabbed my shoulders with the biggest grin on her face and attempted to shake me. "He spoke to me. Did you see that?"

"Uh, yeah. Why is that major?"

She sucked her teeth. "You wouldn't understand." She turned to Teila and did the same thing.

Teila laughed and pushed her away. "Just play it cool, like you don't even care."

"Yeah, yeah. You're right," Bradly whispered as she composed herself.

I put Chana's licorice on the counter and patted my pockets. "Oops. I don't have money."

"I've got it," said Teddy.

"Do you need a bag?" asked the cashier.

"Nope." Chana took the licorice. She nudged Teddy with her hip. I guess that meant thank you.

"You eat sooooooo much sugar." I lowered my voice. "Is that an angel thing? Do all angels that take human form love sweets?"

"Shh . . ." She looked around, making sure no one heard me. "I have no idea what you're talking about, so—"

The man's phone rang.

Cameron and Corey had left. The rest of us were still in the store. We all froze. Except for Parker. No, Parker didn't have a freeze button or an off switch.

Parker rushed to the guy and snatched the phone right out of his hand.

My eyes grew wide. The guy was about the size of two of my fathers. I checked off several reactions in my head that he could have:

- ✓ Snatch it back from him.
- ✓ Yell at him to give it back.
- ✓ Threaten to call the police.

But I was wrong on all counts.

The man didn't say a word as he turned, and then...

WHAM!

His open hand hit the side of Parker's head. Parker fell sideways into a rack of off-brand cupcakes and apple pies, knocking it over and smashing a few.

I think everyone gasped, including the cashier.

"You hit a kid!" Teddy exclaimed.

The guy peeled the phone from Parker's fingers. "He tried to rob me. I'm calling the police."

"No, he didn't!" I thought fast. "I saw the whole thing. You dropped your phone, and he caught it and stood right there."

"That's what I saw too," said Teddy. "Go ahead and call the police, so we can tell them how you attacked a minor." He and Logan helped Parker up. "Bradly, I know you got it."

The two boys held Parker between them and guided him toward the door.

"I sure did!" she said, holding up her phone. "We're live, and as you just witnessed, this grown man just hit our classmate, a thirteen-year-old from Mona Shores Middle School."

The man stood there with his mouth open.

The cashier pointed at Parker. "Stop right there. Don't try to run."

"Let him go. He'll think twice before he tries to do something like *that* again," said the man.

We hurried outside, with Teddy and Logan helping Parker in the lead.

Jasmine stared at him. "Parker, are you okay?"

"What happened to him?" asked Cameron.

"Parker bought us a few seconds by taking that guy's phone," said Bodhi. "And Bradly, that was cool how you said he was from a totally different school."

Bradly did her best to act like it was no big deal that Bodhi complimented her, but there was no hiding that smile or the way her eyes twinkled.

"What happened to your face? Did he hit you?" asked Corey.

The right side of Parker's freckled face and his right ear were red. "Yeah, but someone had to do something. The police were calling him back."

"What if the police call again?" asked Bodhi.

"That's *his* problem."

"Yo, from this day forward, Parker is the man!" said Corey.

"That was a superhero move, right?" Parker replied.

"Why in the world—? Are you really a hairy five-year-old or something?" asked Cameron.

"All right then, superhero." Corey laughed, shaking his head.

Cameron glanced at Logan. "Still no emotion, huh? Did you watch this happen? Do you do anything besides stand around? I mean, except when you're throwing bolts of electricity?"

I stepped between them. "Leave him alone."

Cameron crossed his arms. "I don't trust—"

"Hey, I think we need to get out of here," said Teddy. Inside, the man held his phone to his ear and looked through the glass of the door.

"Run!" Teddy cried out.

We all took off toward the entrance of an alley at the end of the building. We turned there, but I stopped and looked behind me. "Where is she? Ariel!"

I ran back out onto the sidewalk. She was running in the opposite direction. "Ariel!" I yelled.

Ariel stopped.

"You're going the wrong way!"

Her hands flew to her mouth, and she ran back past the front of the store with the biggest grin on her face.

"I can't believe you," I said as I pulled her hand.

We ran down Merrill Ave, past a man walking his dog (he watched us like he knew we'd been up to no good), and through a backyard to another alley. Corey stopped first. We gathered around him, catching our breath.

"Hey, I'm going home," said Jasmine. "I'm right down that way, by the high school."

"Me too," said Parker.

"And me," said Teila.

"Okay, you guys go. It's better if we split up anyway. We'll see you later. And keep quiet about all of this," said Cameron.

"Who are we going to tell?" asked Parker.

"Who would believe us?" asked Teila.

Welcome to my world, I thought.

"Wait," said Bodhi. He pulled off his hat and handed it to Parker. "Give me yours."

"Good idea. Thanks."

Teddy turned to Corey. "Wait. They have cameras in those stores."

"Exactly. That's why we kept our backs to them."

"Spoken like a true juvenile delinquent."

"Former." Corey playfully pushed Teddy, and I was glad because by the way he'd looked at Teddy at first, I thought he was going to sock him in the jaw.

"Yeah, but they could spot you anywhere in this raccoon hat," Cameron said and snatched it off Corey's head.

Corey took it from him and stuffed it in his pocket. "Are we walking the girls home, or what?"

"Yes, let's do that," said Teddy. He wasn't going to let me out of his sight. That's why, even though he lived closer to Justin's house than anyone, he was still with us.

"Chana first," I said.

As we walked, we discussed where Chana would tell her parents she'd been and how she got away.

A block from her house, I saw someone walk out the front door. Once she was on the sidewalk, I recognized her braids.

Chana's mom approached her car and looked up the block, hearing Cameron and Corey horsing around. Then she faced us and stood there a moment before running out of the yard, screaming Chana's name and crying.

She collided with her daughter, almost knocking her back.

"Mom, Mom. I'm okay." Chana hugged her back tightly.

"What happened? Where have you been? Are you hurt?" Her mom asked as she looked Chana over from her feet to the top of her head. "What are you wearing? Whose coat is this?"

Finally, Chana's mom turned to us as if just noticing us. "Did you find her?"

Did we? Are we supposed to say? I wondered. "Yes, ma'am."

"Thank you, thank you, thank you," she said, placing a hand on those who were close enough to touch without releasing Chana.

I hoped she wasn't going to start kissing on me the way she kissed on Chana. Especially with that snot running from her nose.

Ariel squeezed my arm and hopped a couple of times. This was what she'd been waiting to see.

Chana's mom walked her to the house as if she were afraid to let go.

"Uh, did she forget we were here?" asked Bradly.

"Looks that way. Who's next?" asked Corey.

"I can call my dad to take us home, Sheena," said Ariel.

"But won't the police want to question us?" asked Jasmine.

"Her dad's a police officer. He knows where to find us."

"I'm riding with you," Cameron told Corey.

"Drop me off on the way," said Bodhi.

"Me too," said Bradly.

"No. You ride with Ariel," Bodhi replied while pushing her toward us.

"Theo? Are you coming?" asked Corey.

Teddy glanced from me to Logan. "I'll stay."

I pushed him away. "No, you won't. Go. We'll be fine."

He gave me his big brother protective stare that got on my nerves.

"Really. Go. I'll talk to you later."

Teddy pointed as he backed away. "You better."

"I will. Go already."

Ariel put her phone back in her pocket. "My dad is nearby. He will be here any minute."

Somehow, I wasn't surprised. Gleamers seemed to know when they might be needed. "Good. We won't have to go inside and interrupt their reunion."

A siren blared as Ariel's dad's van pulled away from the curb. I watched through the rear window. It belonged to the patrol car with flashing lights that sped up the street and into the driveway. Chana's dad had gotten the news she was back.

We stopped at Bradly's house first. She looked out the van window at her house. "You guys want to come inside?" she asked. "We can hang out like old times."

It had been over a year since I hung out with her. We grew apart as friends do sometimes. We went on summer break, and she came back to school popular, and I didn't. The next thing I knew, she was one of the FIPs and we were sworn enemies.

"I would, but I just want to go home and be with my family," I replied. It was the truth, but there was the whole Logan issue too. I don't think that was even on her mind.

"Okay." She looked toward her house and back at me. "Sure?"

"Yep. See you at school. Wait, your mom's home, right?" I suddenly realized she might not want to be alone after the day we'd had.

"Yeah, I think so. Thanks, Mr. Knight," she said before closing the door. He waited until she unlocked her front door and went inside before he pulled off.

"Is she okay?" asked Logan.

"I don't know. I don't think any of us are."

9

Logan seemed totally unbothered about anything other than the hangnail he picked at the whole ride. That concerned me. Was he used to chaos? No one could possibly go through this kind of stuff every day.

"Sheena," he whispered and motioned with his head. "Her dad."

I was surprised he'd noticed. "Yeah, I know. He's a gleamer."

"There's a lot of them here. In this city, I mean."

"So I'm learning."

Mr. Knight pulled the van in front of our driveway. "Last stop," he exclaimed as if he was a bus driver.

Logan slid the door open, and we both hopped out.

Ariel waved from the front passenger seat. "See you Monday.

"I knew you could do it," she added in what was supposed to be a whisper.

"Not without you," I said with a wink.

There was so much shine behind her eyes and so much knowledge. But it only came out at the most random times. And when it was most needed.

I waved and watched the van pull away, not wanting to turn and face my house. It was totally last minute, but my brain got busy working on answers to what my dad's number one question would be.

I kicked at a chunk of ice beside the walkway and looked at the windows of the house.

"Are you ready for this?" I asked Logan.

"Do I have a choice?"

"Nope," I replied. My dad was going to burst a blood vessel as soon as he saw me. I just knew it.

I stepped onto the first step, paused, and then stepped to the next. I didn't know how long I could delay entering the house, but I was certainly going to try.

This is about to be crazy weird, I thought.

I lifted my hand to try the knob, but the front door squealed open.

You know that part in old movies where you hear dun-da-dun-dun? Insert that. My father's eyes narrowed.

Maybe if I didn't say anything, he'd think he was mistaken about me being there. *I'm invisible. Will it, Sheena. You can do it.*

"Where have you been?"

Welp, that didn't work. Once again, no superpowers.

"Well... What happened was..." My eyes darted everywhere, around the doorframe, to the now tiny scratch on my dad's cheek from his car accident, to the grey and black threads in his brown sweater.

Why hadn't I rehearsed what I was going to say? I mean, I knew what he was going to ask. I should've had an answer ready.

My dad's voice rose. "I said. Where. Have. You. Been?"

That's it, I'm totally grounded. Chana is back, and now I won't see her again for a month. Depending on how angry he was, maybe two. Earplugs. That's what I needed. They would get me through the scolding part of the evening and help me to stay quiet. I never could. I always argued my point. My parents had a way of not seeing my side of things, so I tried to make it clear. It never helped. Ever.

I didn't know how to answer my dad's question. It would only make him madder.

Unexpectedly, my dad's face lit up. He broke into a grin and pulled me toward him. He hugged me, lifting me from the porch floor.

"You did it, didn't you, Baby Girl?"

My head laid against his goatee. It was warm against my cold forehead.

"It's the craziest thing, I don't know whether to ground you for life or hoist you up onto my shoulders and parade you up and down the street as a hero."

"Daddy," I laughed. "Put me down. You can decide on that later. We have company."

"Huh?" He looked around me as he set me down.

Logan raised his left hand. "Hi."

"This is Logan."

My dad cocked his head and raised a brow at me. "I know that already."

"No, you don't know *this* Logan."

Nana walked forward and embraced Logan. My mom was behind her with her fists on her hips. *Oh, boy. She's mad.* You could tell. Locks of waves from her twist-out were shaking even though she stood still.

"You know who I am?" Logan asked Nana.

"Glory be. Yes, child. You're with family now."

He hugged her back, and I felt the release from him as if I could see it. His whole posture relaxed like he'd been holding heavy dumbbells over his head and finally set them down.

I tried to see his face through those big curls. Was he crying? I would've been ugly crying. "Bawww—I have a family! Bawww—I'm not alone anymore! Bawww!" That would've been me.

My mom unclenched her fists, and her hands dropped to her sides. "Mama, I don't understand. How is he family? Isn't he the boy from across the street?"

"This here is Tobias's grandson," Nana said.

My mom looked confused. "But we're not related to Mr. Tobias."

"Yes, we are," I replied. "Tell her, Nana."

"Mama?" said my mom.

"Let's all sit down."

Why does everyone always want you to sit down? Just tell them, I thought, anxious to hear Nana's story.

My dad took our coats, and we walked back to the family room. The scent of tomato sauce and chili powder filled the air. And at the sight of someone's half-eaten bowl of chili on the kitchen counter, Checkers resting on the sofa, and the glowing embers of the fireplace—I was happy to be home. Happier than I would've been if I were in trouble, of course. I wondered if Logan felt the same warmth and safety being there.

We sat around the sectional in the family room, ignoring the game show on the television.

Nana began again. "Mr. Tobias's son, the one they're looking for..."

Logan and I glanced at each other.

"He's my father," Logan finished for her.

"The man that's after Sheena? He's not related to us," said my mom. That last part was an octave higher.

Before Nana could respond, a broadcast interrupted the game show. Luke's mugshot appeared on the screen. His hair was wild, and his eyes were dark and creepy-looking, like the night at that warehouse when he had me pinned against the wall.

The news anchor stated that an anonymous tip led to finding Luke's body in an abandoned house.

One side of my mouth quivered and began to rise. *Grin on the inside, Sheena,* I told myself.

"The police are not ruling it a homicide. Vance Nichols is on the scene right now."

A man wearing a winter coat, unzipped enough for you to see the tie on his neck, stood in front of the brick house. "As you can see behind me, deputies are removing the body from the home. We're waiting on the coroner's report, but right now it seems he may have suffered a heart attack."

A gasp came from my mom. "It's over. It's finally over," she said, more to herself than to us. She looked at my dad.

Logan stared at the floor rug.

"Luke was my nephew," Nana said.

"How?" asked my mom. "But that means—"

"Tobias was my brother-in-law."

My mom's eyes were wide with disbelief. "Mama, why didn't I know this? Sheena, did you know when I took you to the hospital that day?"

I shook my head.

Nana sighed. "I don't expect you to understand, Belinda. But if you take two strong gleamer bloodlines such as ours and bring them together, what can come from them is too great to comprehend. So there are things that must be hidden to protect…"

"What?" asked my mom.

"Me," said Logan, petting Checkers, under his chin.

Checkers didn't usually like strangers. His ears pointed upward and forward, and he gave a soft purr, showing his approval.

"I've been in foster homes my whole life," Logan continued. "My father started contacting me when I was old enough to understand. I'd received letters, explaining what I—uh—telling me about him and the family. After a while, the letters stopped. But I moved a lot over the last few years. I figured he didn't know where to find me. That might've been on purpose, to protect me."

"From who?" asked my dad.

"Him, I think. You saw what he became. I didn't hear from him again until after he was arrested—this last time."

My dad listened intently and rubbed his hand over his goatee. "But you moved in across the street."

Logan shook his head. "No, sir. I was trying to stay close to Sheena. My father believed something was going to happen to her, so he sent me to keep watch."

"But I thought—Didn't he want to hurt her?" asked my mom.

"Not the new him."

"This doesn't make sense," she replied.

My parents fell silent for a minute. Nana and I watched them.

"It's a lot to take in," my dad finally said and stood. "Logan, I guess we'd better call your uncle. He's your next of kin."

I shot up from my seat. "We're his kin. She's his aunt, great aunt," I said, motioning toward Nana. Then I pointed at myself. "I'm his cousin."

"He should be with his closest family."

"But that's us," I said, placing my hands on top of each other over my chest. "I promised. I told—I mean, I said we would take care of him." My voice was rising. "I told him I would keep my promise, and I have to."

"Told who?"

I followed my dad into the kitchen, where he picked up his cell phone from the counter.

"Luke," I blurted out without thinking.

Insert that dun-da-dun-dun again.

I felt everyone's eyes on me without even looking around. It took me a moment to face them. No one blinked. Except for Nana. She turned to the back window, facing my willow. I didn't know what all Nana's gleamer gift entailed, but it was obvious she knew things. I could see it even then.

"Keep your promise," Luke had said as he disappeared with the angels. I was determined to do just that.

I swallowed. "I meant, Luke would want him with family."

My mom stood. "But that's not what you said."

"But that's what I meant," I replied. "I got jumbled up."

My mom walked over. Sheesh, she caught everything. "But that's not what you said," she repeated.

"Where is your mother, Logan?" my dad interrupted.

Whew, thanks for the save, Dad.

My mom's steady gaze left me for a moment and switched to Logan.

"Dead, sir."

"Do you know your uncle?"

"No."

"Who knows where you are?"

"No one."

My mom took her cell phone from her purse. "We need to call the authorities and—"

"Bee, wait a minute. Belinda," said my dad. His eyes met mine.

Could he see what I was trying to tell him? My mom always said my dad and I were just alike. He had to understand. My eyes pleaded with him to let Logan stay.

My dad sighed. "I propose we give all of this some thought for the night. Before Sheena holds her breath until she gets her way or passes out.

"'Why can't I stay up until eleven? Why can't I see an R-rated movie? When I go away to college I'm never coming back,'" he mimicked, and then he filled his cheeks with air, holding his breath.

I scowled. "I don't do that."

My dad let out his breath. "Maybe not today."

"Don't listen to him. That was years ago. I don't throw tantrums," I said over my shoulder to Logan.

"Glory be, that's her all right," said Nana, walking toward us.

My mouth dropped.

"I bet Logan would like to spend some time alone. And maybe a hot bath?" she asked.

He nodded. "Yes, ma'am."

"Come with me."

Logan followed Nana down the hall and up the stairs.

I placed the palms of my hands together as if praying, put on my puppy-dog face, and pleaded to my mom, whining, "Pleeeeeeeease."

My mom threw her hands up. "All right. I give."

I hopped up and down.

"Only because I feel this is some type of gleamer matter. I'll get the spare room together. Later, you and I will have a talk about why a thirteen-year-old thinks she can go wherever she wants, whenever she wants, without asking her parents.

"Jonas, I'll have to give him a set of your pajamas," my mom continued.

"Not my lucky ones," my dad replied.

"And that would be which ones?"

"The ones that cause my basketball team to win when I wear them. You know the ones." He lowered his voice. "With the puppies."

"You and those doggone pajamas," my mom said as she walked away. "I guess I better figure out dinner also."

"Ooo, Mom, Mom! Please make your lasagna," I called after her. "But make it the way you used to before you got all health conscious. You know, without the cheese made out of cashews."

She paused at the room entrance. "Well, you don't seem to have a problem with it in my vegan mac-n-cheese."

My dad made a barf face behind her back.

She pointed at him without looking. "Stop it." She came to my side. "We'll see." She rubbed my arm, kissed my forehead, and walked away again.

They'd left me and my dad alone. I scooted over to him like I was doing the electric slide and hugged him.

"Ah-ah-ah," he said, taking me by the arms and pushing me back where he could look me in the eye. "What are you not telling me, Baby Girl?"

"Why would I—"

We both turned toward the news again, hearing the reporter say Luke's name. I read the ticker on the bottom: Luke Tobias has been found. "In an odd turn of events, the house next door—found to be owned by Luke Tobias's deceased father—exploded today after a natural gas leak. No one was hurt."

"Were you there?" my father asked.

"Were you?" I replied. "I seem to remember something you told me. You're 'the protector of gleamers—of one in particular.' I also remember you saying, 'I always know where you are, even when I don't tell you.'"

He winked at me. "That's right. Because I'm the," we said it in unison, "protector of gleamers."

"So you know what happened?" I asked while walking into the kitchen. I opened the refrigerator, took out the whipped cream, and sprayed some into my mouth.

My dad followed me into the room. "Hey, stop that. Actually, hand it over." He squirted some in his mouth also.

I swallowed. "You didn't answer my question."

"What question?"

I snatched the can away from him. "Daddy, you're eating all of it! And stop ignoring the question."

"What question?"

"I asked you, 'Do you know what happened?'"

"Maybe."

"Then why didn't you help?"

"Which part?"

I looked down the hall to make sure my mom hadn't returned. "The explosion."

"Hmm… seems to me, you and your friends walked away without concussions or major injuries."

"That was you? I did see you standing over me?"

"Maybe."

"What about in the basement?"

"You didn't need my protection. There was a lesson to learn."

"What kind of lesson? That I'm a warrior?"

He grinned. "We don't always know what's inside us, but there's a lot we can learn from experiences. Often, adversity is the best teacher."

"But you could've helped."

"In school, does your teacher help you when you're taking an exam?"

"No. Is that what it was—a test? How could that be a test?"

"You've shown you're ready."

"Ready for what? Does Mom know?"

"No." He tossed me a bag of peas from the freezer. "For your shoulder."

"Thanks." I put the cold bag on my aching shoulder. "Tell me what I'm ready for, because I have so many questions. And Daddy please don't start with the riddles."

He studied me for a moment. "Okay. You're right. It's time you know."

Finally, I was going to get some real answers from him.

"Now, this is serious." He gave me a stern look. "Listen closely. You cannot share this with anyone."

"I won't. I promise."

"Not even Chana."

"I won't."

We both leaned over the counter arm-to-arm, almost head-to-head, as my dad spoke softly. "When the moon meets the indigo sea, then will it hail upon the mountains and rage will inflict the foolish."

Huh? I thought for a moment. *Indigo. Hail. Foolish.* "But that makes no sense at all."

"Exactly. You'll know when you need to know."

"Ugh," I whined. *Here we go again.*

10

I stood inside my bedroom, listening at the door for Logan to leave the bathroom and walk to the guest room.

When I heard him, I jumped away from the door, pounced onto my bed, and back up again.

No sounds came from the hall now. Why didn't I just open the door? It wasn't like I'd never talked to him before. I paced my floor for a moment and pressed my ear to my door again.

A few minutes later, I went to his room. Logan spoke softly to someone. Then the doorknob shook. I jumped back into my parents' bedroom with my back against the wall.

Please, please, don't come in here. I can't explain this. But whoever it was didn't enter the room. Their feet bounded down the stairs.

I started breathing again and walked into the hall.

It wasn't like me to act so anxious, but I couldn't help it. Logan's room drew me like a magnet. I paced the floor in the hall in front of the door, waiting for him to exit. Finally, I heard the floor creak and raced back to my room.

PHOOF!

That was the sound I made when I tripped over Checkers, my shoulder hit the wall, and air release from my lungs. I'd hit the same bruised shoulder I'd fallen on when Mr. Tobias's house blew up.

"Sorry, Checkers," I exclaimed and scooped him up. I laid on my bed on my side, trying not to grimace from the pain shooting down my arm and up my neck.

Checkers looked at me with his greenish-yellow-I-know-all eyes as if to say, *I saw that.*

Logan's shadow approached my door.

"Oh, hey," I said and sat up when he walked in. He wore my dad's light gray t-shirt and dark gray striped pajama pants with beige cocker spaniel puppies all over them. Both hung off him. His hair was still wet, so his normally large curls were just starting to pop up again.

He noticed my amused expression. "Your dad has an odd choice in pajamas." He pointed behind him. "Were you just in the hall?"

"You probably heard Nana. She's older, but she goes up and down the stairs all day. Not old. I mean grandma old." *Just stop talking.*

He grinned. "Yeah, okay. Do you think you should get that?" he asked, hearing my phone dinging.

"I can get it later."

He picked it up from my dresser and handed it to me.

Really, Logan? Do you always go around touching other people's stuff? That's why there are so many germs on cell phones.

I didn't take it from him. Instead, I reached over and unlocked the screen. "Watch this," I said. "I'll tell you what the texts say without even looking." I glanced around the room to the right of me, then focused on my window as I thought.

"Cameron: 'How is your girl?'

Chana: 'What's up, Chica?'

Teddy: Umm . . . 'Did you see the news? I told you, you have a lot of explaining to do. Pick up!' Oh, and probably an angry face emoji.

Ariel: 'Sheena, are you okay?' She'll probably ask if you're okay too."

Logan nodded.

"Oh, and also from Cameron, something like, 'It worked. They don't know we reported it. Corey wants to know where Logan is and if you're sure he's legit.'"

"Wow, almost perfect," Logan said. "Except there's something to the effect of having to bust me up."

I laughed.

"It's cool you have friends."

I nodded. "This is a recent development. I'm not used to having so many."

Logan walked around my room, picking items up and setting them back down, examining every little thing.

"Yep, this is Sheena Kingdom," I said with my hands in the air as if I expected applause.

Logan smirked and kept right on exploring. He picked up a few stones from my nightstand.

"Those are just rocks I collected from Sleeping Bear Dunes in Traverse City. Ever been there?"

"Nope."

He pulled a board from between my dresser and desk and laughed. "What's this? Playdough?"

I was so embarrassed I'm sure my face turned burgundy. "When I was little, I vowed to try every flavor of bubble gum. After I chewed them, I stuck them on there. Notice the neat rows. Some of the labels aren't legible now or have fallen off."

"That's funny."

"Yeah, I've always been different. But can you put that back? It's a little gross, but I keep it and a lot of other things because I'm nostalgic."

"No problem."

"So what do you want to do?" I asked. "Or are you ready to talk about the big elephant in the room?"

"Straight to the point."

"That's the way I am. You'll get used to me."

"Yeah, you're right. We should do that." Logan's hands slid down his pajama pants like he thought he'd find pockets. Then, he held them behind his back.

"Phew, I'm glad you agreed. I thought I'd have to talk you into it. So that thing that happened on the street. It was the M—" I caught myself. I still didn't want to say Murk aloud.

"Oh..." He seemed surprised. Maybe that wasn't what he expected to discuss. "I think it was. It's trying to get stronger. The more we fear, the stronger it gets."

I nodded. "Hey, why does it seem like you're everywhere?"

Logan's head lifted, and his eyes perked. "That's what I mean. I'm not, but what if—I mean..." His hands flew up to his head. "I sound like an idiot. So. Okay. Well, it's umm... Never mind."

I laughed. "I don't know what that was. Slow down."

Logan didn't know it, but I planned for him to spend that evening telling me all he knew about gleamers and whatever else I wanted to know.

"What I was trying to say was, I don't know."

I tried to raise a brow at him like my dad does and squinted one eye.

Logan tilted his head, studying me. "Why is your face like that?"

"Ignore that." I wasn't so good at doing the brow thing on demand. "Hey, have you decided about your uncle?" *Say no. Say no.*

"I don't know. I've never really had a real home. What you have here with your family is nice."

"Yeah, I'm blessed." I looked around my bedroom and into the hall. For some reason, I felt I needed to point out something that wasn't so great, so it didn't seem like I was bragging.

Logan followed me out of the room and joined me under the attic entrance.

"Except for that," I said, pointing at the attic door. "It's scary as heck at night. For the past few weeks, I've thought someone was up there."

Logan looked away. "Someone was."

11

I waited for Logan to crack a smile, but he didn't. "You're not joking, are you? Boy, I know you're not telling me you were in my house?" I whispered-yelled. I paused for a moment. "That explains a lot, actually. How did you get in?"

He shrugged. "It wasn't hard."

"But we have an alarm system. How did you get past it?"

"The code."

I waited for him to tell me more.

Logan shook his head. "I've never lived with my family, and you're here living among a whole city of gleamers. Still, I know so much more than you about us. Your alarm code is your birthday."

"But how would you know that?"

"Parents always use birthdays for passwords and stuff, and all type-one gleamers are born on the same month and day."

"No."

"Yes. Me, my father, his father—we're all born on August—"

I held up my hand. "Wait. I thought I was the last type-one."

"You are. I'm a year older than you."

I grabbed his hand and pulled, marching him into my room.

"What are you doing?" he asked.

"Shh," I said. "Tell me what else you know. I need to know everything. No one will tell me anything but riddles." Checkers purred as I sat. I lifted him onto my lap and rubbed his tan ear. The other one was black, and his face was white. The patches were shaped like squares, reminding me of a checkerboard.

"You first." Logan crossed his arms. "How did you find your gleamer squad already?"

"You can see their gleam?"

"Of course. Can't you?"

"Barely. Really, I just found out that everyone has a bit of a gleam in them, and that I would have some sort of team—or squad, as you called them."

"Yeah, your assignment is not meant to be done alone. You'll need help." He tilted his head. "Why is your guardian visible?"

What assignment? I wondered.

"That, I don't know," I replied to his guardian question. "Chana has always been here. How come you and Ariel know what she is?"

"Ariel, she's a healer," he replied.

"Yes."

"That girl is powerful."

Wait, but wasn't I powerful? *I'm the last gleamer, and a type-one, and a mighty warrior (that's an exaggeration). But all of my gifts haven't even been revealed. And he's going to tell me how powerful Ariel is?*

Logan walked over to my portable speakers. "What is this music?"

"Fleetwood Mac. Good, right? Stevie Nicks is the whole reason I listen to them, though."

Logan stared at me. I'd come to know in my thirteen years that not everyone appreciated good music.

"I have no idea who that is. Do you listen to anything else?"

"Of course I do, but don't change the subject. What I really want to know is what kind of gleamer are *you*?"

"A type-one."

"No, I mean what are your gifts? Because what I saw you do to that chest and to Luke—"

Oh my gosh. Why did I say that? Sometimes my mouth didn't get permission from my brain, and it rattled off without thinking.

I looked at him shyly. "I'm sorry. I didn't mean to bring that up."

"It's okay."

"Then can I ask," I knew I was pushing it, but I had to know, "do you feel bad about your father?"

Logan sighed. "I'm not happy he's gone, if that's what you mean. It would have been harder had I had a real relationship with him. It wasn't easy, and I have to live with that now. But it had to be done. He knew that. That's why he left me no choice."

"Why did it have to be done?"

"Because you're the Angelus—"

"What's going on, guys?" asked my dad, walking into the room like he was a beat cop patrolling the neighborhood.

I fell back on my bed and screamed into my pillow. My dad, in his customary way, interrupted just when I was about to find out something good. I hadn't closed my bedroom door, because it would've been obvious I was in detective mode. Plus, no boy, not even Teddy, had ever been in my room with the door closed. That might get them killed.

"Nothing, just talking about being cousins," Logan said, covering for me. "Is she always like this?"

"Unfortunately." My dad gave him a wry smile. "Hey, downstairs there's leftover chili. But we've also got pizza, with *real* cheese." He pointed to Logan's borrowed pajamas. "You look good in those, Logan."

"Thanks, Mr. Meyer. I was just telling Sheena they're pretty comfortable."

I sat up. "No, he wasn't. He wanted to know why a grown man has puppies on his 'lucky' PJs," I said with a chuckle.

"I did not."

"It's okay, Logan. This is how our family is." My dad popped me on top of the head.

"Ouch!"

"Sheena loves to make fun of me. I guess I'm pretty 'lucky' all the pizza is locked in my bedroom."

"Is not!" I said and sprang from the bed.

Later that night, I lay thinking about the day. Not so much about the bad parts. I used all the willpower I could muster to stay away from those thoughts. But the image of Luke dying kept flashing in my mind. I saw the sparks that emitted from Logan and the intensity of the pain on Luke's face. I'd watched someone die, and the only person I could really talk to about it was Logan.

He couldn't possibly be sleeping. He'd experienced everything I had. My whole team was all probably laying in bed with their hands clasped behind their heads, looking up at their ceilings, just as I was.

I threw my covers back and got out of bed. The furnace clicked on, but that was the only sound I heard in the house.

I slowly opened my door, hoping it wouldn't creak. I stood there for a moment, letting my eyes adjust to the darkness. My family knew I liked the hall light left on, but they'd been turning it off after they thought I was asleep.

It was cooler in the hall than in my bedroom, and I wished I'd thought to put on a robe over my plaid flannel pajama pants and long sleeve t-shirt.

Within seconds, my eyes adjusted to the darkness. I could just make him out—a figure standing there, motionless—a little taller than me and the shape of his hair from his curls.

"Logan?"

"Walk toward me."

"What are you doing standing in the hall in the dark?" I whispered. Then I folded my arms over my chest, thinking he could see my t-shirt that read, *Approach With Caution*.

"Don't move," he whispered back.

I'd never admit it, but I wasn't too good at following instructions. I slowly turned, facing the end of the hall like he was.

At first, I didn't see it. Then it flickered.

That shimmer thing was inside my house.

This is the way the second floor of my house is laid out. When you come up the stairs, my parents' bedroom is directly to the right. It takes up the whole front of the house. Directly across from the stairs is the room Logan slept in. It was used as an office but also had a Murphy bed.

My room is down the hall on the left. Straight past my room at the end of the hall is a bathroom, and next to that on the same side as Logan's room is Nana's bedroom.

That's where it was. On that end, in front of the bathroom, outside of Nana's room.

I slowly lifted my cell phone (yes, I grab it as soon as I leave my room) and pushed the side button with my index finger. The light from the phone made it easier to see the shimmer we'd seen outside.

"What is it?" I asked, breathless.

Logan didn't answer, and I couldn't turn away to see if he was still behind me. I felt something touch me and jumped. It was him, guiding me backward.

Outside his door, we stopped in silence, watching it. Then the light from my phone shut off, and I clambered to push the side button again.

I slowly turned it toward the end of the hall. It looked to me like...

"Nana!"

I charged down the hall. The shimmer dissolved through her bedroom door.

Nana never locked her door, so I turned the knob and rushed in.

"Oh no! No, no, no, no, no!" I repeated in a soft whine, seeing Nana's bed empty and the curves and lumps in the sheets where her body had been. I looked under the bed, and Logan looked in the closet. Though I don't know why we thought she'd be in either place.

Suddenly, I stood and laid my hand over my forehead. "What am I thinking? She's downstairs."

"Or outside," said Logan, quietly.

I walked around the bed and stood beside him at the back window.

"Is—is someone out there?"

The bedroom light flicked on, and I jumped on top of Logan. But he didn't try to catch me, and we fell into the wall.

Nana entered the room, staring at us as if we were crazy. "Glory be, what are you two doing in here?"

"Sorry," I told Logan as I pushed off the wall to stand upright. "I—uh—we were looking for you."

Nana tilted her head. "At this time of night?"

"Yeah, we couldn't sleep. Were you just outside? Doing the whole hedge of protection prayer thing?"

"I'll let you know after you tell me why you were really in my room," Nana replied as she walked over and looked out the window, which I found odd. *Did she think we saw something out there?*

I closed her bedroom door.

"We saw—I don't know what we saw," I told her.

She pressed her lips together. "Both of you? Describe it."

"A light shimmering in the hall outside of your door. Maybe it was a ghost," I said with wide eyes.

"Now, you know your Nana doesn't believe in ghosts."

"Do you know what it was then?" I asked.

"I have an idea," said Logan.

"You do?" I asked.

Nana didn't look afraid, shocked, or concerned. She just sat in the chair beside her bed and listened.

"You know how you can reflect the light off a mirror onto a wall?" Logan explained. "That's what that is. It's not a thing, but light reflecting—"

"What light?" I demanded.

"Not what, but whose."

12

Logan couldn't have possibly meant the light reflected from a person. I must have misunderstood. Like that time my mom said, "don't eat that cookie," but I heard, "eat that cookie". Twice.

"What do you mean, whose?" I asked him. "Look, you need to tell me exactly what's happening here. I want to know everything. Full disclosure, or I play the dad card. What's it going to be? Tell me, or I start screaming for my dad."

He didn't respond.

What was he hiding? "You have the floor, Logan. Come on, spill it."

He ran his hand through his hair. "Where do I start?"

"What kind of gleamer are you?" I know you're a type-one, but it's different.

"Yeah. Protector. Like your father, but different. And yes, I can tell what type he is."

"That makes sense, actually. So how did you get Luke out of prison? That officer didn't even know he let Luke out."

Logan pointed at Nana.

"Anything you want to say to me, you can say in front of Nana."

He shook his head. "No, look."

Nana looked to be fast asleep. I put a finger to my lips, covered her with a throw blanket, and walked around her bed.

Logan followed and whispered, "That wasn't me."

Logan

"Sure it wasn't." I glanced at the picture on the wall next to Nana's door and did a double-take.

That's why I recognized the one at Justin's house. It was almost identical, with the same faded smudge with writing beneath it and everything.

"It had to be you," I continued. "Who else could it be?" I walked into the hall to the attic door, and he followed me. "And why do you keep going up in the attic?" I lifted the stairs and pushed them up, so they bent as the door raised and closed. He must not have closed it well, so the stairs extended. "You don't have to anymore."

Logan looked in the bathroom, and then up the hall and hurried ahead of me to my room.

I marched after him. "What are you looking for?"

He opened my closet doors and looked inside. He looked under my bed and out the window.

"Logan, what are you doing?"

"Your father said you have trouble sleeping. I figured if I show you there's no bogeyman in here, you'll sleep better. You should go to bed now."

"What am I, five? Don't change the subject."

"I'm not. I'll tell you more tomorrow. Promise." He placed his hand on my back and pushed me toward my bed.

My door closed as I turned around. Seconds later, I heard his door close too.

What just happened?

I climbed into bed, confused but satisfied I was starting to get some answers. The next day, I'd make a whole list of questions for Logan and ask Nana about that picture.

My eyes suddenly widened. *The shimmer thing was in my house. It didn't want to hurt anyone, did it? Was it evil? Nana said we were protected, so no evil could get inside. What if it came into my room while I slept? Luke's face as Logan zapped him. He killed someone. But it was so he could save me. Did that make it okay? Mr. Tobias's house blew up! No, don't go there. Nurse Javan showed up out of nowhere—I mean what is going on? Something is very wrong.*

That was the last thought I remembered before falling asleep. I vowed to stay awake all night and figure things out, but my body had other plans.

I awoke and looked at my window, watching the sky turn from a muddy gray to a gray-blue. I'd slept right through the night without any nightmares. Maybe Logan searching my bedroom really did help me relax. I stretched my arms above me and my feet below me and let out a loud wide-mouthed yawn as I wiggled my fingers and toes.

"Time to take on the day," I said and hopped up. This time, I was already in the window and waving at Dingy when he looked out across his backyard. That brought a huge smile to his face.

I ran in place while punching my arms, raring to go. Logan had another thing coming if he thought I'd allow him to skirt around my questions that morning.

"Music," I said and snapped my fingers. I found my earbuds under my comforter, placed them in my ears, and danced around for a minute. My family, Chana (and Teddy

I guess) were the only things I loved more than my music, and in that order. The '70s through '90s music. My dad called me an old head, or was it an old soul, or maybe it was just old. I couldn't remember. Everyone else called it weird.

I grabbed my clothes and ran to the bathroom. If I hurried, I wouldn't miss Logan leaving his room to go downstairs.

In spite of everything, like that shimmer thing being in my house—in my hall, near my room—I was in a good mood. Logan said it was a reflection. Whatever that meant. Maybe that was the first thing I'd ask him about.

When I got back to my room, my stomach growled like a caged animal. I realized the conversation would go much better after a meal. My phone vibrated. I reached for it but changed my mind and drew back my hand.

There were too many voicemail messages and texts. It would take forever to answer all those, "What happened?" or "Are you okay?" questions.

All I wanted that morning was for everything that had been poured into Logan to pour out and flow like a faucet to me. All the gleamer stuff. *How did he know so much, anyway? Man, if I could get my hands on the letters Luke sent him,* I thought.

After hearing my phone vibrate again, I had an idea. I could respond to one of my friends and tell them to pass on the message to everyone else. *But who?*

Ariel.

Chana would usually be my first choice, but she'd object to contacting everyone else, and Teddy would have too many questions.

My thumbs moved quickly over my phone: *Ariel, I'm fine. Will call when I have more time. Tell the team for me.*

My tongue rested against the roof of my mouth. The taste was a bit sour and chalky. "Yuck, I need to brush my teeth." That often happened when I got too busy dancing or engrossed in one of my projects. I'd only washed my face.

Two light taps sounded on my door.

"I'm up, come in."

"Good morning," said Logan as he opened the door.

"Morning. How did you sleep?" I asked while covering my mouth with my hand. A whiff of my dragon breath might ruin his breakfast.

"I slept okay. So, what's the routine around here?"

"There isn't one." I backed up to my bookshelves. I figured that was far enough away from his nose. Unless he had a superhuman sense of smell or something. "Hey, how did you know about Chana?"

He leaned against the doorframe. "Do you have to know everything right now? Can we do this later?"

"Yeah, but just tell me that. Was it her glow?"

"Guardian angels shine differently than you. Let's see... How can I put this? It's like they are outlined in bursts of energy like stars. So, if there was no flesh—"

"You could only see stars or the energy." I thought about that for a moment. "Cool."

"Wait, you don't see it?" he asked, surprised.

"No. Just in her eyes."

"Why is your vision so limited?"

Here we go.

He scratched his chin. "You're kind of in the dark about everything."

"I'm not in the dark." It was true, but I refused to admit it. "Okay, that's enough for now. We can finish this convo later. I'm hungry, aren't you?" I hurried past him and into the hallway.

The television volume was turned up loud in my parents' room like it always was when one of them wanted to listen to the news from the shower.

At the stairs, I leaned over the banister. I could hear my dad talking to Nana.

"Hold on," I said, stopping Logan from walking any further. "This is what you should know about my mom and dad. They represent a united front. Okay? So what one says goes with the other. Don't try to play them against each other. And Nana, whatever you don't think she knows, believe me, she knows. And I don't know how. Oh, and my dad is weird about vegetables."

"Got it," Logan said.

I looked him over. His hair was cool. It was like a loosely curled straight almost-afro. He'd better beware of Bradly.

We entered the kitchen, and I stared at the empty granite countertop. My dad sat at the table, reading an article on his phone.

"What's wrong?" asked Logan.

My arms stretched out to the sides. "Daddy, where's the food?"

He glanced up from his phone. "Good morning, Logan."

"Good morning, sir."

"My daughter has forgotten how to speak to her family when she walks into the room in the morning."

"Sorry. Good morning, Daddy." I went over and kissed him on the cheek. "Where's the grub? I thought you were making breakfast."

"Where's the toothbrush? I thought we practiced good hygiene around here."

My eyes bulged from their sockets. Like they were literally probably on the verge of falling. How could he embarrass me like that in front of Logan? I turned and ran up the stairs and straight to the bathroom.

On the way out, as I dried my mouth on the bottom of my t-shirt, I glanced inside Nana's room. Bed made, throw blanket folded and laid at an angle over the foot of the bed, everything neat and in order. And most importantly, empty.

I stepped as lightly as I could into the room. Our wood floors creaked at the slightest movement, and I could just imagine everyone downstairs looking up at the ceiling if they heard it, knowing exactly what room I was in.

I studied the picture on the wall next to the door. It was dull looking because it was so old. Maybe that's why I'd ignored it most of my life. Yeah, I remembered it now. On the wall at Nana's house. Just outside the kitchen. The house the Murk tore apart.

The scene was more map-like than an image of an old Muskegon. I carefully lifted it off the wall and turned it over. Brown paper covered the back. I'd have to tear it to get to the drawing. Nope. I didn't go around ruining my grandmother's things. I'd just have to ask her about it.

I'd thought that I could take the photo out of the frame and make out the writing at the bottom. I placed the picture above the hook and slid it down so the string would catch, then straightened it. *There. No evidence that I was in here.*

My stomach growled loudly again, and I hurried downstairs.

As soon as my foot hit the landing, I heard a shout.

"SOCK RAT!"

I screamed and jumped back on the stairs while watching the balled white sock fly across the floor and into the door.

Logan ran and picked it up, laughing. "I'm sorry. Your dad made me do it."

I snatched it from him. "I know. This is what I deal with every day."

"Daddy!" I said as I tossed the sock at him. "You didn't have to show him that."

He was still in throes of laughter, holding his side. "Why do you keep falling for it? Did you take care of that dragon?"

"Filter, please. You cannot say stuff like that. Sheesh, embarrassing people all the time." I walked right up to him and blew hard in his face.

"Much better," he said and pushed me away. He tapped on his tablet. "And before you get started again, it's not my turn to cook. But I *am* hungry. Tell that woman to get down here and cook me something."

"Who?" asked Logan.

I grinned. "Ooo, I'm telling you called her 'that wo—'"

"I heard him, Sheena," my mom said, walking into the room. "Tell your father just for that, we're having a veggie scramble for breakfast with egg whites, spinach, asparagus, tofu . . ."

His face squinched up more with each word. "Ma Val, can you help me out here?" He looked at Nana, who now sat at the table. "Don't let her do this to our guest. She's making a bad first impression."

"They're like this all the time," I told Logan.

"You're right," said Nana. "What would you like for breakfast, Logan?"

"The scramble is fine with me."

My mom grinned.

My dad looked shocked. "Just when I thought things were about to change around here, you side with the women? This kid has got to go."

Logan's face fell. "Oh, sorry."

"No, I'm joking."

"Cereal?" asked Logan.

I shook my head.

"Pancakes?"

"Now you're talking."

13

The doorbell rang.

"I'll get it!" I danced to the door, humming a song from my favorite musical. It was on television, and though I wasn't paying attention to it, the song stuck in my head.

I opened the door and crossed my arms. "Teddy, why are you here?"

He frowned at me from the doorstep. "Hello to you too. Are you going to let me in?"

Before I could step aside, he pushed me aside.

I closed the door behind him. "What are you doing here?"

"You asked that already," he said while taking his coat off and handing it to me.

I dropped it. "You know where the hook is."

He picked up his coat from the floor. "It's too early for your attitude. I'm here because you have a weirdo in your house and—"

"Whoa, that's not okay. He's not a weirdo. You shouldn't throw that word around like that."

He hung his coat on the hook next to the door. "Okay, well, some random gleamer. And *you* should answer when your phone alerts and reply to texts."

"Did you think something happened to me?" I laughed. "Are you here to save my family?"

"I guess so." He leaned back, looking down the hall and into the kitchen.

"Yes, there's food," I said. Teddy might have come over out of concern, but it was Nana's cooking that kept him here.

My mom was at the stove, and from the smell of the room, breakfast must have been ready.

"Theodore! Hey!" said my dad. "I like how your afro is growing out. Do you miss your dreads?"

"Not anymore." Teddy nodded at Logan, who sat at the table. "Logan."

"Hey."

"Plate?" my dad asked Teddy while handing one to him.

He pretended to push it away. "No, thank you."

"What?"

"Joking!" Teddy exclaimed with a laugh, taking the plate. "What've we got?" He looked over the stove. "Pancake tacos? Yes! Can I borrow Nana for a few weeks?"

I rummaged through a drawer for forks. "My mom made those."

Teddy walked up to the stove and smiled at my mom. "No fruit in mine, bacon, and eggs, please."

My dad grinned. "That's what I'm talkin' about!"

For a boy who was so concerned about Logan, Teddy sure had a good time playing video games with him in the basement.

Most of the day, I waited for my parents to say, "Well, that's it, Logan. It's time to go," or some rendition of that. But they didn't.

I wanted to pump my fists in the air and wave them like nobody cared, or however the song went. My parents were going to let him stay. I had it all worked out in my head. We'd need his social security card, birth certificate, and immunization record to register him for school, so he could join me at Nelson.

Although, I sort of already had a big brother in my life—Teddy. He wasn't older than me, but he acted like it. I looked forward to having Logan as a cousin/brother as well.

Another gleamer child in the house... Wow, things were about to get interesting.

That afternoon, my dad came home with shopping bags and set them on the breakfast nook table.

"Please don't tell me you bought Logan clothing from a store that sells groceries." I stood on my knees in a chair and took shirts out of a bag.

"I don't mind," said Logan. He looked at my dad. "You really didn't have to do this, though. My things usually come from second-hand stores."

"Tell us about that, Logan. I think Sheena needs to hear this. Maybe it will make her a-ppre-ci-ate," my dad said, with an emphasis on each syllable, "what she has."

Teddy picked up one of the shirts. "I'll take this if he doesn't want it."

I hopped off the chair, grabbed his arm, and pulled him.

Teddy yanked his arm away. "See how she does me, Mr. Meyer?"

"Don't you have someone else to bother today?" I asked and handed him his coat.

He took it from me and put it on. "Why are you so mean? I came to tell you we have a meeting tomorrow after school."

"We who? And why are you just telling me now, if that's what you came here to do?"

"Our team. Everyone's coming over here. And I can't help that you guys are always feeding me."

I rolled my eyes. "Why my house?"

"We figured you were probably grounded since you didn't pick up your phone."

"When people are grounded, they can't have company."

Teddy shrugged. "We thought grounded as in, can't leave the house."

"You guys have some strange ideas of what grounded means."

"See you tomorrow."

I started closing the door. Teddy pushed it back open. "And call Chana back. She's annoying as heck."

"I will, now out."

"One day, you're going to stop kicking me out."

"Yeah, uh-huh…"

"You know you love me."

I shut the door.

14

For the second night in a row, I slept right through without any nightmares. In fact, I awoke refreshed and flitted out of bed, throwing my cocoon of blankets off me. I grabbed my phone, put my earbuds in my ears, and walked to the bathroom, rubbing my hand over my wild hair.

I should've braided my hair and put a bonnet on before bed, but I didn't. We'd had so much fun the day before and well into the night. I didn't even get to question Logan. My dad fired up the grill (yes, in winter), and he even lit the fire pit for s'mores, though we didn't stay outside long.

Now I'd have to spritz my hair with water, brush some gel along my hairline, and pull it back into a ponytail for the day.

I stood in the bathroom mirror staring at my reflection. "I know you," I said to the girl staring back at me with a smile on her face. There were no thoughts of the Murk or that shimmering thing, or Luke. "It's going to be a good day," I told myself.

Since I didn't wake during the night, I really had to pee. Thank goodness I didn't dream I was using the bathroom again.

Two seconds after I sat on the toilet, the bathroom door opened.

"I'm in here," I screamed.

"Oh, sorry," Logan said from the other side of the door. "I didn't know anyone was in here. You should lock—"

"Can you close the door?" I screamed.

"Yeah, sorry," he said, slamming it closed.

"Oh my gosh," I mumbled, covering my face with my hands. "There's a half bath on the main floor and another full bath in the basement!"

Logan waited until he heard me heading downstairs before he came out of the guest room. He apologized again. "I didn't see anything."

"Don't worry about it. I have to get used to having someone else in the house."

Nana had been the first person up, as usual, and stood in the kitchen stirring a pot of grits when we walked in. Logan had never had them, so I couldn't wait to see his reaction.

"Good morning, Nana."

"Good morning, Nan—uh, what should I call you?" asked Logan, a little embarrassed. I noticed he avoided calling her anything the day before.

"Valerie or Auntie. Whatever you're comfortable with."

"Auntie Valerie."

I leaned over the counter. "Nana, I meant to ask you, what's that picture on your wall that you brought from your house?"

"Which one?" she asked, sprinkling cheese into the pot.

"The old one of Muskegon."

Her bun was undone, and her braid hung down her back. I walked over and rebraided the end.

"That's exactly what it is, Muskegon."

"But where did you get it?"

"Glory be, that thing's old, sweetie."

"But you brought it with you. It must have sentimental value," I said.

"It does. It was passed down to me from family."

"But there's more than one."

She turned to me. "How do you know that?"

"Nana, the pot!"

Grits popped all over the stove and counter beside it. That's why my mom never let me make them. I burned myself good once.

"Sheena," my mom called from upstairs.

"Finish what you were saying," said Nana.

"I will as soon as I come back. Coming," I yelled up to my mom.

"You said there are more than one. How many are there?" Nana asked as I hurried away.

"I don't know, Nana."

By the time I got back downstairs from helping my mom with her hair, I only had time to grab my things for school and a few pieces of bacon. There's always time for bacon.

My mom and I had gotten into a little disagreement because as she applied her mascara, I asked her if I could wear some. A lot of girls in the eighth grade wore mascara.

"It'll make my eyes pop," I'd told her.

"I'll give you a pop," she'd replied while gliding the tip of the wand along her lower lashes. "Ask your dad if you can wear mascara."

That had been the end of the conversation. I knew how my dad felt about me wearing makeup. "You don't need it," he'd say. "My genes make you naturally gorgeous."

Now, I grabbed my coat and hat. "I'll see ya later, Logan," I said and hurried out the side door.

"Don't worry, Sheena. Us boys will be fine," said my dad.

Somehow it didn't feel right leaving Logan behind. In the short time he'd been with us, I guess I'd become attached.

My mom was already waiting in the car, and I hopped in the passenger side. She backed out of the driveway, and I looked up at the house. I don't know why. I guess I expected Logan to be there waving like Dingy or something.

When we pulled up in front of the school, Ariel was in her usual spot near the bicycle racks, waiting for me. But this time, she wasn't alone. Bradly, Teila, Cameron, and several others from our lunch crew were with her.

Ariel saw us, pointed, and waved.

"Looks like the gang's all here," said my mom.

"Yep. Looks like it." I stared at my mittens for a moment.

"Are you okay, Sheena?"

A car horn beeped behind us.

"Oh, cut it out!" my mom yelled while looking in the rearview mirror. She turned back to me. "What's on your mind? Is it Logan?"

I leaned over to her, inhaling her shea butter scent, then placed my lips against her cheek and blew.

Her hand flew up to the side of her face. "Sheena! You're getting too old for these raspberries." She laughed and frowned at the same time.

I hopped out of the car as she wiped her cheek.

"Have a good day, Crazy Girl."

"Love you. Bye." I shut the car door, then made my way to the sidewalk and joined my friends.

"There she is," Ariel said.

"Why are you guys all out here? Aren't you cold?" I asked.

They spoke at the same time.

"Waiting on you, since you can't call a person back."

"Of course we're cold."

"We didn't want to miss you."

Ariel looped her arm through mine.

"Where's Logan now?" asked Cameron.

"At my house."

"He spent the night?"

"Yep."

We all walked inside with them chattering away.

"Where is Chana?" I asked.

"Right there," said Cameron.

When I saw Chana's two curly afro puffs, I forgot about everyone with me, the kids in the hall, and the teachers. And I know I must've had the silliest grin.

Chana stood leaning against my locker, swiping at her phone. Two beaded braids hung in front of her face. Her nails were freshly polished with pink and purple glitter, and she wore a new coat. She couldn't wear Corey's forever, and Principal Vernon probably destroyed hers.

As if having the same thought, we did our bestie gesture, crossing our arms up high and bringing them down. Then we leaned toward each other, clasping hands and laughing.

"These two," said Teddy as he walked up.

Chana nudged me. "What's up with you? I almost disowned you for not responding to my texts."

"Oh, I—"

Chana laughed. "That was a joke. I'm not mad that you've been ghosting me. I know there was a lot going on at your house. At mine too, with the police and everything."

My throat collided with my chest. I couldn't swallow if I wanted to. Why hadn't I checked on her? Her disappearance and rescue had to have been a mess to explain. Did she remember to say we found her on the street after she got away from whoever kidnapped her? Of course she did. Angels didn't forget stuff.

I covered my face with my hands. "I'm such a bad friend."

"Sheena, it's okay. Really. Okay?"

I nodded.

"Ooh, you used gel today. I see you," Chana said.

I grinned and glided my hand from my hairline back to my ponytail, "Do you? Am I shining?"

"We've talked about this. Please don't try to use slang. Shoosh, before someone hears you."

"But I'm Gucci."

"We're Gucci," said Ariel.

Chana rolled her eyes. "Oh my gosh. You guys are killing me."

I laughed so hard because, honestly, I had no idea what it meant. I'd only heard kids say it, and I knew it would get on Chana's nerves.

"Hey, Sheena, you were good in the play," a boy said in passing.

"Thanks."

"See? And you didn't even want to do it," said Cameron.

"But I did."

"And he's right. You *were* good," said Chana.

"You weren't even there."

"So you think," she whispered.

"Okay, break it up, double trouble. We all need to meet to discuss everything," said Cameron, stepping between us and pushing us in opposite directions. "After school."

"Tomorrow?" asked Bradly.

"No, today."

"Why the urgency?" I asked.

Cameron gave me a serious look. "Because I have to tell you something."

"What?" asked Teddy.

"Just be at her house," Cameron replied, motioning his head toward me. "It's not like I didn't already tell you this."

The first bell rang, and everyone scattered.

As I predicted, the day started out rather well. No one mentioned anything during the first two classes.

Third period, I sat at my desk, flicking my pencil back and forth and waiting for Chana to arrive.

"Superpowers. Superpowers. Superpowers," Parker whispered behind my ear. I swatted at him, and he jumped into the desk beside mine.

"Why are you harassing me, Parker?"

"I'm just trying to remind you of—"

Chana walked up the aisle, just as the bell rang. "You're in my seat," she told Parker.

"Remind me of what?" I asked.

She waited beside her desk with her hand on her hip. Then she crossed her arms.

"Okay," he said and stood. She placed her books on the desk, sat, and stared up at him. "Well?"

"Parker, what is it?" asked Mr. Haleigha from the front of the room. "Please tell the class what is so important that you can't wait until after class to talk to Sheena."

The students in the seats in front of us turned around and watched Parker.

"We're all anxious to hear," said Mr. Haleigha.

Parker could've said nothing, apologized, and took his seat. But he looked at me like I knew what he was talking about. "Are you sure you want me to?"

"Go ahead. I don't know what you're going to say."

"I don't think…" Cameron said from the seat behind Chana. "No. Do you. I'm staying out of it."

Parker lowered his voice. "I was just asking Sheena when she's going to give me superpowers to battle evil."

Chana, the class, and even Mr. Haleigh laughed. "Get to your seat, superhero."

"Into the Gleamerverse," Parker whispered.

"Don't make me punch you," said Chana.

When Mr. Haleigha turned his back, I passed Chana a note that said, *Logan walked in on me in the bathroom.* I'd doodled a shocked face beside it.

"No way," she laughed. "Did he see you taking a dump?"

"No. Gross. He was on the other side of the door."

"Oh, he smelled it then," she said, holding her nose.

I swatted at her playfully. "I wasn't pooping."

Mr. Haleigha cleared his throat. That was the cue for us to stop talking. And we stopped. I didn't want him calling my parents again, so they could get on my case about being too close to Chana. "You see each other every day, and you're always on the phone. Why can't you wait until after class to talk?" my dad had asked the last time. I didn't have an answer for him.

Mr. Haleigha walked across the front of the room. "Who would like to give their report first?" He said it like it was the most fun task we could imagine.

"Did you do it?" Teddy asked from the seat behind mine.

"No, but my grade is safe. I can do this in my sleep." I raised my hand, but Mr. Haleigha looked all around me. He wouldn't even meet my eyes, ignoring me when he asked an ecology question.

The way my life was going, for all I knew, I was invisible and didn't know it.

"Theodore, get up here," the teacher said.

Teddy scowled. "I didn't raise my hand."

Mr. Haleigha tapped two fingers at his temple, and then pointed them at Teddy. "You didn't need to. I knew you wanted to go next. It was written all over your face. 'Mr. Haleigha, please pick me next,'" he said with a grin.

Teddy grunted softly so only those around him could hear it and stood.

Chana stuck her foot out, and he kicked it.

"I hope you trip on the way up there," she said and stuck her tongue out at him.

"Well when it's your turn, I hope you have explosive diarrhea in the middle of your report." Teddy replied and walked to the front of the class as slowly as he could.

"I don't have to do mine today because I wasn't here," Chana said, but Teddy wasn't in range to hear her.

At the front of the room, Teddy bowed. A couple of girls giggled.

He cleared his throat and tugged at the neck of his sweatshirt. "Your carbon footprint is the amount of greenhouse gasses in the air because of what you do in your home. Like turning on the heat—but we'll freeze without it, I'm just saying. Many of us get rides to school, and you know how long the drop-off line is and how long it takes. Cars emit exhaust and greenhouse gases and pollutants. It's better to take a bus because it's one vehicle instead of many, but it emits greenhouse gases too."

"I'll give you a greenhouse gas," someone said and farted.

I covered my mouth to stifle the laugh that exploded from others.

"Could you not!" Chana exclaimed.

"Hey, that's enough," said Mr. Haleigha. "Continue, Theodore."

"Factories that make all the stuff we like produce greenhouse gasses. Our TVs, our phones, games—you get the idea. Oh, I forgot, large factories make our fast food, and then have to transport it long distances. That generates more emissions. You've seen the semis full of milk or trucks carrying ice cream bars or whatever."

"Anything else, Theodore?"

"Umm . . ." Teddy scratched his chin and glanced at me.

I quickly balled up a piece of paper, pointed at it, and threw it over my shoulder.

Teddy's head lifted. "Yeah, uh, recycling reduces emissions."

"Yes!" I exclaimed.

Mr. Haleigha put his hand up, telling me to stay quiet.

"How?" he asked Teddy. "Don't look at your paper."

"Recycled stuff does not emit greenhouse gases as it decomposes or is burned, so it's better than mining new materials."

Mr. Haleigha neared Teddy and lifted his hand for a high-five. "Good job."

Teddy slapped his hand and did a fist pump in the air while raising his knee. Then he pranced to his seat, looking relieved.

"Nice," I said over my shoulder.

"Thanks for the clue," he whispered.

"Does anyone have anything to say about Theodore's report?" Mr. Haleigha asked the class.

I raised my hand and waved it back and forth as I tapped my feet quickly on the ground.

"Could you please act like you're thirteen?" asked Chana. She pointed over her head at me.

"I was trying to give someone else a chance to speak first, but go ahead, Sheena," Mr. Haleigha finally said. "Before you spontaneously combust or something."

"Finally. We're killing our planet!" I exclaimed and slammed my hand down on the desk.

"Here we go," someone said as I stood.

"Overfishing, cutting down trees, and building everywhere."

"Sheena?" Mr. Haleigha tilted his head.

"Yes?"

"We've moved on to talking about your carbon footprint. That's what Teddy's report was about."

"I know, but you hadn't called on me yet."

Mr. Haleigha sat on the edge of his desk. "Well, in what you just said, you've touched on the subject. You're off to a great start. Bring it home. Tell me how you believe we can reduce our carbon footprint. You do agree we need to reduce it, right?"

"I thought I just did. I said we need to stop cutting down trees."

"Elaborate."

"Well, umm…" I thought back to a website about the environment I'd browsed. "I read that beef from cattle from places like Brazil hurts our planet. The cows there graze on land that used to be forest. Deforestation contributes to carbon emissions, which affect climate change. Did you burger-eaters know that beef causes more damage to the environment than any other food product?"

The class clapped.

"That's my bestie!" Chana exclaimed.

"Go Sheena, go Sheena," said Cameron.

"Well done," said Mr. Haleigha. "Are you a vegetarian?"

"No."

"So are you going to stop eating meat?"

"Who said anything about that? I had bacon this morning."

Everyone laughed.

Parker shot up from his seat. "If you get bitten by a Lone Star tick, it can cause a severe allergic reaction to red meat and meat products. Just put one of those on everybody."

Some of the class voiced their disagreement. Others laughed.

"Have a seat," Mr. Haleigha told him.

"Just so you know, Theodore's report is exactly like mine. So there's no reason to hear the same information again." Parker said as he sat.

Mr. Haleigha called on the next student, and as she stood, I noticed Logan peeking in the door window.

15

How does he always know where I am?

"Logan's out there," I whispered to Chana.

She looked at the door. "He is? Go. See what he wants."

I raised my hand.

"Yes, Sheena?" Mr. Haleigha said.

I pointed to the hallway and mouthed. "Bathroom."

Mr. Hallelujah nodded. I called him that because he let me leave without a question or a speech.

I hurried out. "What are you doing here?" I looked up and down it, making sure no one would hear us. "And how did you know where my class was?"

Logan shrugged. "I was a student here looking after you, remember?"

"Uh, that was just last week. How could I forget, Mr. Fake Student?"

"Middle school is the easiest place for a fake middle school student to blend in," he said with a grin. "I came to say goodbye."

My heart dropped. "Where are you going?"

"My uncle is waiting outside."

"Your uncle from Ohio?"

"Yes."

"Wait, who called him?"

Logan frowned. "Sheena..."

I couldn't accept it. "No, you can't go. I promised your father you'd be taken care of."

"You're still keeping your promise. I'm being taken care of, just like you said."

I stamped my foot. "I meant at my house."

Logan put his hand on my shoulder. "Sheena, I want to know more about my father. More than *I* know about my father. Do you understand? The good and the normal stuff. My uncle can tell me about that. What he was like as a kid, what his favorite foods were, how he laughed."

He could do that over the phone, I thought but kept it to myself. "I get it. Can you wait though? Class will be over soon."

"Sheena, I need to tell you something. About us." He squeezed my shoulder.

"Us?"

"Gleamers. Things aren't—they're not what they seem."

I held my hand up, brushing his aside. "Gleamer here. I think I've learned that already."

"Yeah, but I'm trying to say, because, well, there's good and evil…"

"Yes."

He rubbed his neck, looking flustered. "In the battle of good and evil. There's good, and then there's evil."

I put a hand on my hip. "That's usually how it works."

"Well, the two can come from the same place."

"From God?" I raised a brow. That didn't sound right.

He shook his head. "Yeah, but, no, that's not what I'm trying to say. There's more."

"Logan, you aren't making any sense. Just like the other night. Whatever it is, just tell me. We're family. You can tell me anything."

I looked inside the classroom door window and met Mr. Haleigha's gaze.

Logan cleared his throat. "I have a—"

"Mr. Haleigha is coming to the door. I have to go back in. Don't leave, okay? You're gonna wait?" I said quickly.

"I'll wait."

I managed a grin. "It was fun, right? Except for the, you know . . ." I said and went back inside the classroom.

Teddy leaned over his desk. "What happened?"

"He's leaving."

He looked satisfied to hear it and whispered the news to Cameron.

Every few minutes, I looked over my shoulder at the clock on the back wall, waiting for the bell to ring. And when it finally did, I was the first one up from my desk and out the door.

Logan was gone.

For the first time in as long as I could remember, Principal Vernon didn't stroll into the cafeteria in his perfectly starched and pressed suit, looking us over, and waving at or joking around with students. Nor did whoever took his place. Didn't they know we needed someone to stop us from throwing food, standing on lunch tables, or doing any of the other things Principal Vernon corrected us on?

Every time someone walked through the cafeteria doors, I noticed from the corner of my eye and expected to see him there. I guess I'd miss *that* Principal Vernon, the one who seemed to look out for us. Not the evil one.

We all gathered around the two tables we'd pushed together at lunch.

My day had taken a turn for the worse with Logan leaving. I was sad, disappointed, and frustrated. Logan hadn't even answered my questions. Now, he was gone.

Chana sat chatting while stuffing french fries into her hamburger. You would've thought nothing bad had ever happened to her.

"Double trouble, back in action," said Cameron as he sat with his tray.

"Do you get new clothes every single week?" asked Bradly.

"Don't hate. I can't help that I've got style. Chana, how are you back here already?" he asked, reaching for a fry.

She slapped his hand.

"Yeah, I can't believe your parents let you out. My parents wouldn't want me out of their sight," said Teila.

Chana smirked. "I told them, 'Look, you two—'"

I laughed. "You didn't say that."

"Yes, I did," Chana insisted. "'Look, you two,' I said. 'Either let me go to school, or I'll blast Sheena's music all day'."

My mouth dropped open.

Chana shoved me. "Just joking."

"Can you believe we did it, though?" asked Jasmine. "We all saved someone."

"Who?" asked Chana.

"You."

"Oh. Yeah. Right."

Jasmine sighed. "It was so hard not to tell my little sister."

"You better not have," said Cameron.

"I didn't." She turned to me. "Sheena, I've been meaning to ask. What exactly is a gleamer? I mean, I kind of know, and I know what I've seen, but how does that happen?"

"Can you guys stop using that word?" I set my sandwich on the table. "It's just like the definition of gleam. To shine brightly, especially with reflected light. Gleamers reflect the light of—"

Teddy held up his hand to stop me. "I've got this. They reflect the light of the sun."

"That's son. S-O-N. Not S-U-N," said Cameron.

"What 'son' would that be?" asked Parker.

Justin jabbed him and pointed at the ceiling. "The *Son*, who else?"

"I was kidding, sheesh!"

"But the light is reflected from the Son to angels, and then to her. Her gleam is super bright," said Ariel, pointing at me. "Blinding."

They all stared at me for a long moment, and I put my hand up, shielding my face from them.

"I don't see anything," said Bodhi, squinting at me.

"Why can Ariel see it?" asked Jasmine.

"I wanna see it," said Teila.

They were all so hungry for information—biting into their sandwiches and burgers, staring at me.

"Yeah," said Justin. "How did it start?"

I shook my head. "No, I don't think so."

"Why are you acting so secretive?" Justin asked. "We've already seen so much."

"No, you haven't, and not all of you were there."

"You can tell them, Sheena," said Ariel. "They're your team."

Ariel was her usual happy, jolly self. But today, because of the mood I was in, that was about to get on my nerves.

It wasn't her fault I was irritated. It was Logan's fault. He should've demanded to stay.

I took a deep breath. "Okay. This is going to go fast, and don't ever ask me to repeat it. Because I won't. And don't interrupt."

"What did I miss?" asked Tyler, walking up to us with his tray.

"Shh... Just sit down," said Cameron. He pulled out the chair next to him and Tyler took a seat.

They were all so focused on me, flames could've been shooting up around us and they wouldn't have noticed. I probably could've told them anything, and they would've believed it.

"Okay." I swallowed. "I saw an angel. I watched it save my dad."

"No way," said Tyler.

"I met an old man," I continued. "He could see them too."

"Can you see them all the time?" Tyler asked.

"No."

Chana glared at him. "Didn't she say, 'don't interrupt'?"

"I wasn't here for that part."

I ignored him and moved on. "The old man told me about the evil that's fighting against us. It's trying to control kids to create a hopeless evil generation. It killed him. You guys know about everything after that. Pretty much." I looked at the faces of Tyler and the rest of the new members of the team. "Most of you."

"So you were born like this?" Jasmine asked.

"Yes. But I didn't know about it until this school year."

"Ooo... Have you guys heard?" asked Tyler. "Principal Vernon is missing."

"No, really?" asked Cameron with a grin.

"Could you stop smiling?" asked Chana.

Teddy, Cameron, Justin, and I glanced at each other but didn't say anything.

"Who's taking his place?" asked Parker.

Tyler shrugged. "I don't know."

Ariel, sitting to the left of me, was having a conversation with Bradly. Then I watched her remove her hand from Bradly's wrist. They both stood with their trays. I grabbed mine too and followed them, listening.

"I'll be right back," I told Chana.

"Do you believe in God, Bradly?" asked Ariel as they walked toward the bins.

Bradly shrugged. "When I'm at church."

"That's the only time?"

Bradly looked over her shoulder at me. She knew I'd heard her. "When I'm with you, I believe in everything. Even in myself," she told me.

"Why not at home?" I asked.

"God doesn't live at my house."

I almost dropped my tray. Why would she say something like that?

Bradly's eyes were tearing. "You would know that if we didn't have that break. And then, you acted like you didn't know me anymore."

I frowned. "Me? You didn't want your new friends to see you talking to me."

"That's what you thought? That's why we became enemies?"

"No. I mean, I still spoke to you—sometimes."

"Really?" Bradly said with an attitude.

What did I do? This whole thing seemed to come out of nowhere.

"Sheena!" said Cameron, waving me back over to the table.

"What?" I asked over my shoulder, finally breaking away from Bradly's stare.

He pointed at me. "Your house after school."

I went back to the table. "Not right after. I have to make sure it's okay."

"Five o'clock? Can everyone make it at five?" asked Cameron, looking around at everyone. "Because I really need to tell you—well, *show* you something."

"Hey, don't invite everyone," I whispered.

"Why not?" he asked.

"Not the kids who ran or who were so frightened they ducked."

Cameron nodded, slowly understanding. "That's what's up. Got it, Angel Girl," he said with a wink.

I turned back to Bradly, but she and Ariel were leaving the cafeteria.

16

The day passed like a dream. Logan was gone, Bradly called me out on not being her friend, and I didn't get anywhere near all of my questions answered.

Chana's father picked us up after school. I was silent all the way to my house. "See ya later, Chana. Bye, ID," I said and closed the door.

I ran up the front stairs and into the house. I didn't even stomp the snow off my boots first. Someone had left the front door unlocked for me. I quickly closed and locked it, and then pulled off my boots, allowing them to drop wherever they landed, and threw my coat and hat on the bench before storming down the hall toward the family room.

"Here it comes," I heard my dad say.

"What category?" my mom asked.

"By the sound of the stomping, oh, I'd say a category five hurricane."

"It?" I asked, marching into the room.

My dad sat with my mom on the couch. Nana was in her armchair next to the window.

My dad's arm flew up. "There it is."

"You called me an 'it'?" I demanded.

"No, I meant 'it' as in what you're going to say."

"Well, I've got a lot to say. Why did you make Logan leave?" I knew my tone was a little over the top, maybe even out of line, but I figured, what did I have to lose? I was the . . . what did Logan call me? The Los Angeles Bellatron? Plus, I had a valid point.

"We told you the other night it was best for him to be with family," my mom said calmly.

I threw my hands in the air. "Oh my God! You don't listen to me. I explained that he—"

"Don't you dare take the Lord's name in vain!" Nana's words shot across the family room. She even stood.

My hand flew to my mouth. "I meant OMG..."

"It means the same thing, and you know it." Nana glared daggers at me. "What has gotten into you?"

"I'm sorry, I'm just saying..." My eyes began to water. It was rare for Nana to take that tone, and I didn't like being the cause of it. "We should've helped him. We were what he needed."

The next thing I knew, I was full-blown crying, and about to blow snot bubbles.

"Aw, look at you." My dad got up. He came over to me and rubbed my arms. "I didn't know it meant this much to you, Baby Girl."

I nodded. "I'm trying to do what's right."

"Dry your eyes. You know what? It's going to be okay."

I sniffed as he handed me a tissue. "It is? You're letting him come back?"

"No."

"No? This isn't fair!" The tears started up again.

Dad sighed. "Cry all you want. You'll pee less."

Tea flew from my mom's mouth, and I think her nose too. She choked and coughed.

"Ugh! Why is there always a tropical storm raining over my life?" I turned and ran down the hall and upstairs to my room.

"And there's the drama," my dad replied.

"Jonas..." I heard my mom say.

I flung myself on my bed and vowed never to speak to him again.

Minutes passed, and my mom didn't come up to console me. I blamed my dad for that too. He was probably all, "Leave her alone, Bee. She's just spoiled and having another tantrum. You only make it worse going up there". I'd heard him say something to that effect before when I eavesdropped.

As usual, I got all worked up, and when I calmed down, panic set in, jolting me out of my funk. *I yelled at my parents! Again! What's wrong with me? Doesn't the bible say something about your life being shortened for disrespecting your parents? Ack! I'm going to die! But I was only trying to make them listen and see my side of things.*

Maybe my dad took pity on me because I was so distraught. I covered my face with a pillow and screamed into it. My mom, dad, and Nana deserved an apology. Why was I so bad at expressing myself calmly?

The cry left me "tuckered out," as Nana would say. I fell asleep and woke to my phone vibrating. *4:55.* "They're here."

I ran to the bathroom, poured some mouthwash into the cap, and tossed it into my mouth. I swished it around, held my head back, choked from almost swallowing it, and spit it out. That would have to do. I twisted the cap back on and ran downstairs.

"Mama Bear!" Chana exclaimed. I watched them from the landing.

My mom gave her the biggest hug. I was almost jealous.

"Look who's awake," my mom said. She *had* checked on me. I was suddenly embarrassed about the thoughts I'd had.

Chana gasped. "What happened to your hair?"

I patted my head. "I just woke up."

"Bathroom. Now," she said, pushing me toward it.

"Hold on a minute, Chana," my mom said while putting her arm around me and guiding me into the living room. She gave me a firm look. "The only reason I'm letting you have company is because I know how strongly you believed Logan should live with us. We're going to have a talk about this later, okay?"

"Okay," I replied. I knew what was coming. One of my mom's attitude adjustment talks, and me having two write out how I could've handled things better.

After I was presentable, meaning after Chana had put my hair in a fresh ponytail, we waited in the foyer until everyone else arrived, including Corey. Then we went to the basement.

"So what is it you couldn't wait to tell us, Cameron?" I asked.

"Put that cue down. No pool right now. We're not here for games," he told Justin.

"Sounds serious," said Chana.

"It is serious. Sheena knows what's coming. She's acting like it's nothing. So we won't worry?" he asked.

I didn't agree nor disagree.

We spread out, sitting on the floor and around the sectional sofa.

"What are you talking about?" asked Teddy.

"Okay, you know how you and Chana have your YouTube channel?" he asked me.

"What YouTube channel?" asked Bradly.

"They'll explain later," he said. "Just listen for now." He lifted his cap and turned it backward. "After I found out about your channel, I set up a site where teens could talk about whatever they were dealing with."

"Like a forum?" I asked.

"Yeah, like that. Look." He held up his phone, and we all squeezed in to look at the screen.

"I can't see," said Ariel.

"Just give me the site address. This is a smart TV." I turned it on, entered the address, and handed the control to Cameron.

Over the fireplace, a girl with a short blonde haircut and long bangs that swept to the side of her face to her chin appeared on the screen. She wore a black turtleneck top. She looked about fourteen or fifteen years old. The room was dark around her.

"I hear voices sometimes," she said. "Telling me to hate my mom or not to do anything she says…"

"Voices? No, that girl's crazy," Justin said. "Who knows how many wackos are going to post on there."

"Shh . . ." Bradly hissed at him.

The girl on the screen continued, "My parents think I'm schizophrenic. I have to see a therapist now. It's not like that time I thought I saw a Pokémon."

Justin stared at Bradly. "See, she's crazy."

"Don't make fun," said Jasmine. "Mental health is not a joke."

The girl's eyes filled with tears on the TV. "I made the mistake of giving in to it and it turned me against everyone. I almost destroyed myself and my family. I think that's what it wants."

She kept pointing at the side of her head. "It's not me. Not my voice. It's something else—something pushing me. It's evil."

"She's not crazy. She's telling the truth," said Teddy. "That's exactly what I experienced."

"This is proof. It's not over." Corey said from his spot on the couch. "That's what Cameron's trying to show you. All this time, the Murk has been under the radar, building its army of kids again." He stood and motioned to me. "Can you zoom in?"

"I can on the laptop," I replied while opening it.

"Why? What's wrong?" asked Cameron.

We followed Corey's finger to a corner behind the girl.

"What is that?" he asked.

"It's the back of her—her reflection in a mirror," said Teddy.

"No, that looks like a shadow."

We no longer watched the girl, but the corner of the screen. Until the shadow disintegrated like smoke being wisped away in the wind.

BAM!

We all jumped, hearing the basement door slam.

"I didn't forget. I know I'm late, but I'm here," said Parker as he ran down the stairs.

"Does anyone else have chills?" asked Bradly.

"What's that?" asked Justin, pointing at the treat in Parker's hand.

"Sheena's mom just gave me the best waffle I've ever had. It's on a stick. And check this out, there's a hotdog in the center," Parker replied while chewing.

"No way, she gave you a waffle pop?" Justin asked.

"Actually, that's sausage in the center," I told him. "She's meal-prepping for my dad."

Justin hopped up, and Teddy followed.

"Hold that thought," Justin said. "We'll be right back." They disappeared up the stairs.

"Seriously?" said Cameron with his hands up. "Did you not see that? We need to figure out what we're going to do."

"Wait. First, let's talk about what we saw *you* do," Bodhi said, turning to me. "I've been waiting two days to discuss this."

"It's obvious. She's like Elsa," said Jasmine.

"Seriously? From the movie?" Bradly said. "She is not like Elsa."

"What are you, Sheena?" Bodhi asked.

I bit my lip. "Something no one believes in."

"And her?" Bodhi pointed at Chana.

"She's a person."

Bodhi frowned. "But that chest was taking something from her."

"The life force we all have." I made that up, but it sounded pretty good to me.

"Hey, look at this," said Chana, lifting the laptop. "We're trending."

"No way. Do you know how many views you have to have to trend? Let me see," said Teila.

"If that's the case, we're going to need to rebrand you," said Bradly while messing with my hair. I knocked her hand away and moved closer to the laptop, reading the YouTube comments.

I can't remember stuff.
My parents think something is wrong with me.
I remember you. I was there.
There where?
This is stupid.
There's something out there. We are not alone.
Like Aliens?
I was in a dark place. I feel better now, thanks to you.
"We helped someone," said Ariel.
"What does that say below it?" asked Cameron. "Guys, read that right there."
I'm going to take you back.
"Who posted that?" asked Corey.
Chana peered at the screen. "It doesn't say."
"But that's impossible." Teila shook her head.
"Shut the page down," I said.
"Why?" Cameron asked.
"If that's the Murk, we're leading it to them."

17

"I don't get it," said Teila. "There's an entire world out there. Why do you think it's doing so much damage here? What is it about Muskegon?"

"It's Sheena, isn't it? It's because she's here?" asked Justin.

Jasmine unzipped her backpack. "It's like Stephen Woodruff's book." She pulled out her copy. The pages were filled with sticky notes of all colors.

"Someone's been doing some research," said Teddy.

"A lot of what I'm reading is so similar to what's happening, like the Murk read this book."

"That doesn't sound right," Justin said.

"Anyway, it talks about a city full of people with remarkable gifts." Jasmine opened the book. "Good people that helped the whole world."

"What happened to them?" Ariel asked.

"The dark force Stephen Woodruff talks about in the series destroyed most of them."

"Is that a coincidence?" asked Justin.

Cameron grabbed the book. "Let me see that."

I listened to my friends going back and forth, round and round with their theories. As I watched them, one thing was suddenly clear to me. It was just as Nana told me. A type-one gleamer was close to someone who would do something great one day—maybe something that would change the world. That person was right there in Muskegon. And if my assumption was right, he or she was right there in my basement. That's what the Murk was after. Ridding the world of that kid and whoever could stop the Murk from reaching them. All the while, it continued with its mission to create a hopeless generation.

I exhaled heavily and looked down at my trembling hand. Chana grabbed it and rested it on the sofa.

"There's something else," said Cameron, lifting the television remote again. "I didn't want to start with the worst."

"There's something worse?" I asked.

Cameron nodded and went to a site that showed video footage of some kind of rally. "This is live streamed."

The video quality was poor, but we could see the teen who stood on a makeshift stage over everyone else.

The boy's hair was shoulder length. He couldn't have been more than sixteen. The way he spoke was familiar. But it was what he said that made the hairs on my neck and arms stand on end.

"Who is this guy?" asked Teddy.

"I don't know," I replied.

"What's he saying? Turn it up," said Corey.

Cameron turned up the volume.

The boy's voice boomed. "They don't understand us. Acting like we're the enemy, but we're the future. We're the ones who have to fix what they destroy. Us. We are the light," he said with his fist raised.

A room full of teens applauded him and cheered, shouting his name—Phoenix. He looked around at them and his eyes flashed red.

"Oh my gosh," I said, holding my chest.

"What?" Jasmine asked.

"It's found someone to work through."

"How do you know?" asked Teddy.

"His eyes." That was all I was willing to explain.

Everyone sat in silence, watching.

Phoenix glanced off-stage. "Allow me to say hello to a friend, would you?"

"Go ahead, Phoenix!" a girl with a high-pitched voice shouted.

He turned to the camera. "Hello, Sheena. And may your vision be true."

Chana and I shot up from our seats. Everyone turned to me.

"Oh snap," said Justin.

"He—he—he just said my name." I clenched my hands into fists.

"Stay calm," said Chana. "Don't lose faith," she whispered. "It's a scare tactic."

"Why did he do that? How did he know?" asked Parker.

Corey paced the floor, repeatedly pounding his fist into his hand.

"I think Sheena needs to wear a cam at all times," said Bodhi.

"Sheena, remember what I told you about power?" asked Ariel.

I nodded. *Something about me acting like I have no power. But he said my name.* How do you move on from that?

I couldn't take my eyes from the screen. "Turn it off."

Cameron glanced at me. "We need to hear—"

"I said, turn it off!"

18

I closed my eyes for a moment, slowing my breaths, clearing my head and silencing my emotions. My friends waited and when I looked at them, I saw it. A light shone over one of them, revealing the one who would do something great one day. A smile covered my face.

"What's the secret?" asked Bodhi.

"What secret?" Jasmine asked.

Bodhi looked at me with curiosity. "You're not freaking out."

"What will that help?" I asked.

"No. She is. Just not around us. Anyone would be," said Bradly.

Teddy leaned on the back of the sofa. "I don't get it. Why is it always kids? Why isn't this whole thing an adult problem?"

Nana's voice came from the back of the basement. "Because you're the future."

We all turned to her.

She stood near the stairs holding a laundry basket. "You can twist the heart of a child. Young and impressionable kids. Plant seeds in their minds that determine their growth." She walked up the stairs without another word.

"Does she know about all of this?" asked Cameron.

"I don't know." Of course, I lied. Nana always knew.

"Sheena, in that house, in the basement, you said we were something like you," said Justin. "Sparks of light floated around us. How did we do that? I mean," he lifted his hand toward the screen. "We may be needed again."

I shook my head. "I don't know."

"That's too many 'I don't knows', young lady," he replied, sounding like a father reprimanding his child.

"Well, you need to figure it out, Angel Girl, because we've got big problems," said Cameron.

"*She's* got big problems. This kind of stuff should not be on an eighth grader's radar," said Bradly. "I'm just sayin'."

"What *are* you saying?" asked Teddy. "You keep making these comments. If Sheena has problems, we have them too."

Moments like this reminded me of why he was my second best friend after Chana.

"Raise your hand if you've had nightmares," said Bradly.

Everyone except Ariel and Chana raised their hands.

"Chana, tell the truth." Bradly gestured at her. "You more than anyone should have them."

Chana lifted her chin. "If I had them, I would say it."

Bradly closed her eyes. "I've had whole reenactments, and I can't even tell anyone about them."

"You can tell us," said Chana.

Cameron walked over to Bradly. "This is hard for all of us. It's supposed to be. If it were easy, anyone could do it. But I believe we have a destiny to help Sheena." He looked at the black screen. "And help other kids and shut this guy down."

"This is the cancel culture. Let's cancel him," said Corey.

"How are a bunch of thirteen-year-olds supposed to take down an organized group?" asked Bradly, opening her eyes. "This is too big."

Corey shook his head. "It's not. You're making it big."

"Don't say that. She's right. It *is* big," I said. "I'm sorry about your nightmares. If it wasn't for me, you guys wouldn't know this stuff exists."

Bradly stared at me for a long moment. Then her gaze drifted to the floor. "I guess it's better that we do know."

"Does that mean you're in?" asked Cameron.

"Okay, yes. I'm in, I'm in," she said. Although the way she said it, I was sure she was trying to convince herself.

Cameron enclosed Bradly's head in his armpit.

"Stop it!" she exclaimed with a dry laugh.

Corey stuck his hand out, and each person put a hand on top of his. Mine last.

"So we're all in. We're going to do this?" asked Teddy.

"What are we doing?" asked Parker.

"Whatever Sheena needs us to do to stop the Murk and this guy," Corey said pointing at the screen.

That evening, after staring at the floor for an hour listening to my mom's lecture, I stayed out of everyone's way. Especially Nana's. I'd disappointed her, and it tore me up. I didn't even say goodnight before bed. I went to my room and closed the door.

In the middle of the night, I awoke to someone shaking me.

"Sheena," a familiar voice whispered.

"What's going on?" I asked, looking up and trying to focus.

"You were having a bad dream. Those were some crazy noises you were making."

"Logan?"

He nodded. "You're okay now. Go back to sleep."

My parents brought him back?

I turned over and went back to sleep. When I awoke in the morning, I remembered seeing him and went to his room. His Murphy bed was pushed into the wall so that it looked like a bookcase. *He's already up.* I hurried downstairs.

"Good morning most wonderful parents in the entire world. I love you guys. Where's Logan?" I asked, looking into each room.

"Is she awake? Sheena?" my mom said from the family room.

I entered the room, and she came up to me.

"Look at me."

I faced her with a grin. "Where is he?"

"Can you see me?"

"Of course, I can."

"You're not sleepwalking. Where do you think Logan is?"

"Here in the house. Hiding."

My dad stood from the sofa and placed his hand over my forehead. "She doesn't have a fever. Why would you say that, Sheena?"

"I saw him."

"Hold on." He picked up his phone and dialed. "Hey, good morning. This is Jonas. Yeah, hey. Is, umm… Is Logan around?" He was silent for a minute and then handed me the phone.

"Hello?" said Logan.

What was happening? "Logan, hi. I just wanted to say hello."

"You don't sound like yourself."

"No, I'm okay. It's just…" I turned away from my parents and whispered, "I thought I saw you."

"Sheena—"

My voice cracked. "It was a dream, I know. I'll call back later." I disconnected the call. I was so embarrassed. But my parents didn't say another word about it. Instead, they talked about breakfast while glancing at me every once in a while.

I was glad they didn't rub it in. At the same time, I knew what I saw, and planned to prove it.

After school, I had Chana come over. She and my mom went through their whole mama bear routine. I watched and waited, but their gushing was going on forever.

Finally, I pulled Chana away. "Mom, we're going upstairs. We'll see you later."

"What did you do that for, Mrs. Rudeness?" asked Chana. "And why are you in such a hurry?"

"I'm not."

"You're practically dragging me!"

At the top of the stairs, I let go of her hand, walked down the hall, and stared up at the attic door.

"Oh, I get it." She walked up to me. "You called me over because you're still afraid of the attic. We're facing our fears today, are we?"

"Yep. Hoist me up."

Chana intertwined her fingers, and I placed my foot on them.

"I was kidding, actually," she said. "I thought you were over that."

When I jumped, she lifted me higher. I grabbed the handle and pulled down, so the stairs would unfold.

"Not exactly. I've never gone up there." I glanced up the steps into the darkness. "You're giving me the courage to do it."

"Then I'll go first," Chana said and climbed the steps.

I followed her and shined my phone along the wall until I found the light switch and flicked it on. There were boxes and plastic storage bins up there, a bedframe, and an artificial Christmas tree box.

Chana walked to the back. "There's some good junk up here. You guys could have a killer garage sale this summer."

"We don't use the word 'killer' in this house," I replied.

"Oops. Totally understand and never saying it a—gain," she said slowly, stopping at the far end of the room.

I walked up behind her. "Well, as far as I can see, there are no ghosts up—oh my gosh, he wasn't lying."

There was a cot on the floor with a blanket on top, crackers (no wonder we had mice), my Sailor Moon cup, empty wrappers, and a map of Muskegon.

"Who wasn't lying?" Chana asked.

"Logan. He said he'd been sleeping up here to watch out for me."

"Here? I mean, up here? In your house?"

"Yep."

"How many days has Logan been gone?"

"Three."

"Sheena, this cup is wet."

I picked up the pink plastic cup and looked inside, although I could clearly see the droplets from the ground. *I knew it!* But that didn't explain how we called him in Ohio.

WHAM!

I dropped the cup. Chana and I grabbed hold of each other, hearing the attic hatch shut.

"You—you should go check it out," I told her.

She clutched my arm. "Why me? It's your house, warrior."

"Well since we're bringing up titles, you're the guardian. Handle it."

"Listen, it's quiet. I think it's okay," said Chana. "That could've been your mom or dad. No one knows we came up here."

"Good point."

We ran back to the door, pushed, and the stairs descended.

Chana nodded at me. "See, we're not locked in."

I was relieved, but only for a moment. "Did you hear that? Someone is running."

We hurried down the stairs.

"Do you think Logan is back?" Chana asked as we entered the hallway. "Why would he have to hide?"

She followed me downstairs, then past the front door and into the living room. I held my hand out for us to stop there. We listened but didn't hear anything.

"Someone couldn't just live in your house undetected," she said.

"Logan did," I whispered.

We looked around the room. If the person had gone any further, they would've run into my parents or Nana.

"There's nowhere to hide in here."

Drapes hung open in front of the window, letting in the little sunlight we had that day. They were tall and heavy, hanging from just below the ceiling.

I traced them to the floor and pointed. "Since when do drapes have feet?" I whispered.

Chana placed her pointer finger on her lips, made scissor fingers with her right hand and curled them, walking them across her left palm.

I nodded. We tiptoed over to the drapes without making a sound. Chana mouthed, *One. Two. Three.* Together, we reached for the drapes.

"What are you doing?" asked Nana from behind us.

Chana spun toward her, but I couldn't stop. I had to see who was back there. I snatched the drapes away from the window and gasped.

19

I was blinded a moment by the shimmer Logan and I had seen outside and, in the hall, outside of Nana's room. In the blink of an eye, it was gone. There wasn't a person there, although I could've sworn I saw the outline of a body. Sneakers lay on the floor. I knelt and picked them up.

"I've been looking for those," said my dad, walking in. "Where did you find them?"

"Did you guys see that?" My hands shook as I handed the shoes to my dad. "I know you saw it. Chana? Nana, why are you breathing so heavily?"

"Because you startled me."

Chana grabbed me, laughing with her back to the adults. She winked. "They didn't get the joke. Ha! You got me, though. Up or down?"

"Huh?"

"Where are we going?"

"Oh, up to my room."

"Fix those curtains," said Nana.

"Yes, ma'am."

Chana and I turned back and straightened them out. My dad and Nana left the room, and I started breathing again.

"Did you see that?" I whispered.

Chana held her finger to her lips again, and as I looked outside one more time and then at the curtain, the shimmer reappeared. Tiny this time. Expanding on a corner of the window. It glowed and disappeared.

I looked closer. The brown edge of something stuck up out of a crack between the window and the sill. My nails were too short to grab it, but Chana's were long enough. She used them like tweezers and pulled out an old piece of paper.

"Look at this. It's really old," said Chana, handing it to me.

"Come with me," I said and led her to Nana's room.

I held the paper against the wall under Nana's painting. "Look, it's this picture but without the smudge."

We both read the words that had been covered on the other photo. "The path of gleamers."

Chana looked at it closely.

"What is that?" I asked, pointing.

Chana squinted. "Something below ground. Downtown."

"But why would the shimmer lead me to that?"

"What shimmer? Are you keeping secrets from me again?"

I stared at her. "You didn't see it?"

"No. What did you see?"

I sat on the floor while Chana sat on my bed, twisting the front of my hair into Bantu knots. As I flinched and grimaced (I couldn't help it, I was tender headed.), I told her all about the shimmer thing Logan and I had seen.

"I think Nana knows about it," I said.

"Why would you say that? You're being paranoid."

"No, I'm not. Every time I've seen it at home, Nana appears out of nowhere. And this time she was out of breath."

"You think Nana was in the attic?" Chana asked, sounding unsure. "How old is she again?"

"I know it sounds crazy. I haven't worked it all out yet. But something's up. And it has to do with that light, and these prints, and Nana."

"And you," said Chana. "You're the one seeing the light thing. You said Logan told you it's reflecting someone's light, right? Whose light? Nana's?"

"Wait a minute. Reflecting. That's what I said, right?"

"Yeah."

I rushed over to my desk, opened my journal, and flipped through the pages. "Here it is. Look, I wrote down exactly what Ariel told me. We reflect light from angels. Like with the sun and rainbows, she was saying."

Chana raised a brow. "Excuse me?"

"You know Ariel, she has a way of explaining things."

"So what are you saying?"

I met her gaze. "I'm saying this shimmer or whatever is being reflected from a gleamer."

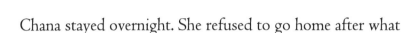

Chana stayed overnight. She refused to go home after what I told her.

"I have to see this for myself," she said.

It almost didn't happen. My mom was all, "It's a school night." So I had to pull at her heartstrings.

"Mom, this is our first sleepover since Chana disappeared. She could've died. I'd thought I'd lost my friend forever. Remember what it did to me? Just this one time? Pleeeeeease?"

At first, she stood her ground. Later that evening, she came up to my room and said, "This one time."

Chana and I had a plan to keep an eye on the attic throughout the night. We were like real detectives staking out the hall. We even had snacks and drinks, though my pantry didn't come close to containing all the goodies that Chana's did. We had more of a charcuterie board with cheese, fruit, crackers, cured meats, pickles, and chocolate pudding. If only we could've had thermoses of coffee. That would've made us legit.

Chana had first watch, but I couldn't sleep, so we waited together. She sat in the doorway with her back against the frame, looking up and down the hall from time to time. Nana was asleep. We checked. If she left her room, we'd see her.

At midnight, we switched places. Chana went to sleep, and I rolled my desk chair over to the door. I sat facing the hall with a flashlight in one hand and my cell phone in the other. The house was quiet. I yawned and laid my head back against the doorframe, fighting to keep my eyes open.

Before I knew it, it was morning. I awoke late and had to hurry to get to school. Ariel didn't wait for me outside like she normally did, and I didn't see Chana or Teddy at my locker. No one was around until lunchtime.

My friends and I sat at our lunch table, watching the cheerleaders march into the cafeteria in their red and black uniforms. Bradly and Teila were front and center, holding their poms at their waists.

Cameron sat on the edge of the table, trying to stick his finger into Justin's sandwich. We were all laughing.

"Whoa-oh," went the rapper on the song the cheerleaders danced to. Everyone stood and went "whoa-oh" with them every few seconds. Then, with each "whoa," the cheerleaders stomped to the left with their knees bent and shot their right arms up at an angle. Ariel, in her cardinal mascot uniform, did the same thing.

"Get it, Ariel," said Teddy.

"She's getting better, isn't she?" I said.

Chana danced next to Teddy, purposely bumping into him, knocking him off balance.

Bradly winked at Bodhi. He watched with a blank face.

Everyone was out of their seats and cheering by the end of the routine. When the song ended, one of the cheerleaders shouted about the game that afternoon, and we all cheered louder. They'd do the same during the next lunch period, hyping everyone up.

"That's what's up," said Justin, as he and Cameron slapped hands.

"Grand Haven Academy doesn't stand a chance against us," said Cameron.

The cheerleaders marched out together, and Ariel pointed at our group and wiggled her finger.

"Me?" said Cameron.

She nodded.

"I'm eating. Why does she want me to come with them?"

"Maybe they need your help with something, Mr. Team Captain," said Teddy.

Cameron sighed and dusted off the front of his jacket. "My work is never done," he said before following them out.

I felt a tap on my shoulder and turned, looking up at Ariel holding her lunch tray. "Scoot over, please, Sheena," she said.

"Ariel, how did you—" I turned and watched Cameron jog off. *If that's not Ariel, who is it?*

Before I knew what I was doing, I leapt from the lunch table, ran across the room, jumped into the air, and came down hard on the cardinal. My charge knocked Bradly into the door frame, but I'd tackled our mascot to the ground with a knee to the stomach.

"Sheena, what is wrong with you?" Bradly screamed.

"She must be off her meds," one of the FPS said.

Cameron stood over us. "Why did you do that?"

"This isn't Ariel," I told him. I turned to the person. "Who are you?"

The person didn't respond, so I yelled again and pulled at the head of the costume. It took some effort, but it released after a few hard tugs.

"No!" I exclaimed as I scrambled back on my hands and feet.

He hadn't changed. His features were still handsome as if he weren't made of pure evil. But then, his eyes flashed red.

"Sheena Meyer," he said slowly. "Did you miss me?"

Drake. It can't be.

Before I could speak, move, or pee my pants, he disappeared. And I awoke. For real this time. I panted for a moment, then sprang to my feet.

I shook my hands like I was trying to shake slime off them as I paced my bedroom floor, trying not to wake Chana.

Calm down. Calm down, Sheena. It was just a dream. That's what my mom would tell me. And I knew it was, but why couldn't I stop trembling?

I didn't sleep another wink that night. I went out into the hall and looked up at the attic entrance. It didn't scare me anymore, but I kind of wished Logan was up there.

When Chana awoke, I was already dressed for school.

"Did I oversleep?" she yawned and spoke at the same time.

I turned from the mirror over my dresser and applied lip balm. "No. I got up early."

"Did you see anything?"

"Nothing."

"So what am I wearing today?" she asked.

I pointed at the outfit I'd laid out on my bed for her. We wore the same size.

She eyed it over. "There is no way I'm wearing that."

"Why? It's exactly the same as what I'm wearing, jeans and a sweatshirt. What's wrong with that?"

She got up and grabbed the scissors from my desk. "Can I cut some holes in the jeans? My legs need to breathe."

"Don't you dare."

She sucked her teeth. "Okay, what about the sweatshirt?"

"No."

"Fine. I'll wear my coat all day."

I did a double-take. Was my sense of style really that bad?

The day dragged on at school. By lunch, I just wanted to lay my head on the table and sleep.

"Are you okay?" asked Chana as we listened to the chatter of everyone around us.

"Just tired."

"You look it. I told you I would take the next watch last night, but you wouldn't let me."

"Yeah, I know," I replied and pushed my sack lunch away. I'd barely eaten any of it. Just as I folded my arms on the table to lay my head on them, I heard familiar music.

"Whoa-oh!"

The beat of the music grew louder. My head spun towards the entrance of the cafeteria.

It was like déjà vu. The cheerleaders marched into the cafeteria with Bradly and Teila leading them.

"Whoa-oh," went the rapper on the song they danced to. I looked around at everyone as they stood and went "whoa-oh" with them every few seconds. Then, with each whoa the cheerleaders stomped to the left with their knees bent and shot their right arms up at an angle.

"This isn't happening," I whispered.

Ariel, in the cardinal mascot uniform, did the same dance moves.

"Get it, Ariel!"

My head snapped toward Teddy. Chana stood and danced beside him, while playfully pointing at the cheerleaders.

Bradly winked at Bodhi.

I slowly stood. *Oh no.*

My heart was pounding almost as loud as the bass of the music in my ears.

Everyone was out of their seats and cheering. The music stopped and one of the girls shouted about the game that afternoon. The cheerleaders jumped, kicked their legs high, and threw their poms in the air.

I knew what was coming next.

"That's what's up," I said along with Justin, as he and Cameron slapped hands. "Just like the dream."

Everything seemed to be moving in slow motion now.

The cheerleaders marched out together, and Ariel pointed and wiggled her red gloved finger.

"Me?" said Cameron.

She nodded.

"Why does she want me to come with them?"

"Maybe they need your help with something, Mr. Team Captain," said Teddy.

"Watch my food," Cameron said and followed them out.

"Yeah, I'll watch it," Justin replied while eating Cameron's fries.

I felt a tap on my shoulder and turned, looking up at Ariel.

"Scoot over, please," she said.

My head was spinning.

"Ariel, how did you—"

I turned back toward the doors. *My dream… It was a warning!*

I ran across the room, jumped, and came down hard on the cardinal's back, knocking Bradly into the door frame and tackling the cardinal—who I was now sure was Drake—to the ground.

He tried to get away, but I pushed him onto his back.

A muffled, "Get off me! I said, get off of me!" came from the mask.

Somebody pulled at me. Then, Cameron and Teddy tried to get me off him. I could hear them telling me to let go, as I pulled at the mask.

Chana screamed my name while reaching for me.

The head finally came off, and I stared at the red face of a boy from the basketball team.

He scowled. "Somebody get this crazy girl off me before I hurt her."

"Try it," said Cameron. "And see what I do to you."

20

For probably the fifteenth time this year, I sat in the principal's office looking around at the degree certificates and plaques on the walls. But these had a new name on them.

The room no longer smelled of furniture polish but of a clean-scented air freshener. The sound of a small air purifier blowing from the corner was soothing like white noise. If someone didn't come in soon, they'd find me asleep.

A woman walked into the room. "It's nice to meet you, Sheena," she said. She didn't sit behind her desk, but in the seat beside mine, which she turned to face me. She held out her hand, revealing a charm bracelet at her wrist. "I'm Mrs. Garcia."

Mrs. Garcia was probably a little older than my parents, short, and wore a blazer and long skirt with boots.

I stared at her hand, hesitant to take it. "Nice to meet you," I said as I shook it.

Thank goodness a door didn't open behind her eyes like it did with Principal Vernon. I didn't see any of her life.

"But it would've been nice to meet on better terms, correct?" she asked pushing her long dark hair behind her ear.

"Yes."

She was nice, caring. But so was Principal Vernon. She could be a fake too.

I knew the routine. Was I being bullied? Why did I attack him? Is everything okay at home? Detention. At least Chana wasn't involved this time. Still, my dad was going to have a fit. Why did I have to believe a stupid dream anyway?

"The jailbird is home," my dad said when I walked in from school. He pulled the curtains back and waved at Chana's dad before he drove away.

"I'm not a jailbird."

"You're going to be. We got a call from the school today."

"Sheena, did you attack the mascot?" asked my mom.

I held my hands up. "Mom, wait. It's not how it sounds. There's a perfectly good explanation for what happened."

"Was Chana involved?" she asked.

"No, just me."

My dad held out his hand. "Let's hear your excuse while you hand over your phone."

"I'll leave you to it," my mom told him and walked away. *Seriously?* I handed him my phone.

He put it in his pocket. "Okay, Sheena. What happened this time?"

"Wait. Daddy," I looked around him and lowered my voice. "So you know how you like golf?"

"Yes. What does that have to do with anything? Did someone swing a club at you?"

"No, but listen. So you know how I watch it with you sometimes, even though I'm bored out of my mind, but I do it so I can spend time with you, and you teach me the terms?" I said all of that in one breath.

"Yes," he replied with his hands on his hips.

"Well, you know that mulligan thing that excuses you so you can hit the ball again after you've done something wrong? You get a second chance. Like that time when you—"

"Ho, ho, ho, wait," he said, checking behind us to make sure my mom wasn't within earshot. "Keep your voice down. That time I what?"

"Dented Mom's car. But look, the mulligan thing in pro golf—"

"That's in casual golf, not pro."

"Oh."

"So what are you saying?"

"I call mulligan."

"A free do-over," he replied as he eyed me.

"You're the one who taught me to defend myself. And—and Chana wasn't involved. And I apologized to him."

"Him? Did you take on a boy? And without Chana this time?"

"Yep."

He rubbed his hand over his goatee, trying to hide his smile. "You have detention."

"Yes. See, I'm already being punished. Maybe we can let this one slide?"

My dad gave in. I could see it on his face before he said anything. "This one time."

"But you said they can have a mulligan every nine holes."

"This one time," he repeated, then he handed me back my phone.

"Yes, sir," I said with a grin. I put it back in my pocket and hugged him. "Where's Nana?" I'd expected to receive an earful from all three of them.

"I don't know, someone picked her up."

"You don't know who?"

"Nana is a grown woman." He shrugged. "She can disappear without me knowing. You can't. Go and ask your mom."

I went into the kitchen and found her at the table. "Where did Nana go?"

"She went downtown to the library. She'll be back soon," my mom said.

"Aww . . . I could've gone with her." I put my knee on the bench, leaned over the table and reached for an orange. I looked out the window. "What is that?"

"Daddy!" I screamed.

I ran to the front door, and he met me there. I flung it open. My mom was right behind us.

"Checkers!"

Checkers was outside on the sidewalk, and I could now see that his head was stuffed in a half-opened can of tuna. The ridges on one side would've cut into him.

My dad ran down the front steps without a coat. "How did this happen?"

"I don't know. I just looked outside and saw him. I don't even know how he got out here." I pointed at the can. "And that isn't ours. I've never seen this brand of tuna."

He hurried away and came back with a flat-head screwdriver, hammer, and can opener.

"What are you going to do with those?" my mom asked.

"I'm going to have to figure it out."

I stared at the tools. "Be careful. Don't hurt him."

"Bee, take Sheena inside," he instructed.

Who would do that to a cat? Especially a sweet one like Checkers. Yes, he hunted mice and acted like a cheetah on the Serengeti when stalking birds from the windowsill, but he was a good one.

My mom brought me into the house. Five minutes later, my dad carried Checkers inside.

"I got him. He's a little frightened, but I think he'll be fine."

"What do you think happened to him?" I asked as my dad handed Checkers to me. I held him close to my chest.

He shifted his tools to his other hand. "He got into someone's trash."

"And dragged the can home with his head in it?"

He set the tools on the counter, then handed me my jacket. "Get your coat on. I want to take him to the emergency vet by the supermarket to make sure he's okay."

Checkers was fine. But no matter what anyone said, I believed someone put that can out there to trap my cat. Something like that changes you. You see the world differently. At least I did. I'd gone from being cautious about my surroundings to DEFCON I.

Just before bed that night, my doorknob jiggled. I stared at it, not sure who was on the other side.

My mom's voice sounded through the door. "Sheena, why is your door locked?"

I stuffed the old map print I'd been studying in my drawer and pulled my sweatshirt over my head. "I'm getting undressed." I unlocked the door and opened it, revealing my tank top and jeans.

"Oh, okay."

"Did you want something?"

"Nope, just making sure you're all right."

"I'm fine."

Unexpectedly, my mom hugged me tight. My arms hung at my sides.

"You're not okay, are you?" she asked into my hair.

My mom wasn't a gleamer, but she could sense things where I was concerned. I hugged her back. If I didn't, she'd only worry about me.

"There's a lot on my mind. That's all," I said. It was the truth. She squeezed me one more time before letting go.

"Okay," she said again and left the room, closing the door behind her.

The knob clicked as I turned the lock.

"Sheena, you locked it again." My mom's voice was muffled behind the door.

"I'm taking my pants off," I replied.

At our house, it was against the rules for me to lock my door, unless I was dressing. Something about if there was a fire and I was unconscious, and they had to get me out. Another time, my mom said something about an idle mind. She didn't want me sitting in there thinking all the time.

That night I broke both rules. I did a whole lot of thinking about what was happening, about that map, and about the boy who knew my name. And I dreamed about Drake. I also locked my door before bed. I didn't want an imaginary Logan wandering in again.

I knelt at the side of my bed and prayed for my friends and for answers and fell asleep feeling positive everything was going to work out. But I ended up having one of the worst dreams yet. At first, I attributed it to what happened to Checkers. But it was more than that.

In the dream, I floated in heaven. Only, it wasn't exactly heaven. It was just like what I'd seen when I collapsed on Mr. Tobias's street, but with more detail. I was in the sky, watching a battle taking place between good and evil. And although I could see angels, I couldn't quite make out what the evil was. But it was swift.

I was only watching like you would watch a movie or a television show, but then something flew at me. I tried to dodge it, but I felt its impact as a hot blow knocked the wind out of me. A flash of light came with the collision. I flew backward, and an angel I didn't recognize caught me from behind without even touching me. I was knocked out but could still see what was happening. The evil thing headed back again for a second blow. I could feel it. But the angel shielded me, fighting on my behalf, as I floated helplessly.

I awoke feeling like I was still floating and like my bed was spinning.

I grabbed my head. *What is happening to me? I'm paranoid, thinking Drake is back. Now I'm feeling like I was actually in a heavenly battle?*

I tiptoed down the hall to Nana's room and slipped inside. "Nana," I whispered.

She didn't stir. I took the Lumen from her drawer and sat on the bed beside her. At least if she woke, it wouldn't look like I was a thief (although how could I steal what was mine) or snooping. I stayed right in the open where she could see me.

Even without Ariel's star to unlock it, I could see the thickening of the pages in the back of the Lumen. Another indication that the Murk grew stronger. Was that what the dream was telling me? Would there be another battle?

I set the Lumen on Nana's mattress and sat on the floor, leaning back against the bed.

"Where are you when I need you?" I asked. "Where is my help?"

I sat staring at the dust bunnies under the dresser.

A soft voice swept over me. "I am as close as your breath."

My eyes grew wide.

"There are no sounds, but there is great communication."

21

I hopped up and ran to my bedroom. "I hear you. I hear you," I said, looking up at the ceiling and every corner of the room. I fussed at myself, *What are you doing, ask your questions.*

"What is that shimmer thing? What's with these dreams? And who tried to hurt my cat? What am I supposed to do?" *Was that everything?*

I waited. I sat at my desk, looking out the window, and waited. I stood at my window, looking up at the stars in the night sky, and waited. I sat on my bed, and then laid back and waited, but I heard nothing further.

The next morning, the doorbell rang while I was putting on my socks. I hurried to the top of the stairs.

My dad was already at the door. "Alien child, what are you doing here?"

Ariel chuckled. My dad always called her that because she said the most off-the-wall things to him.

"Ooo, so I don't have to? Awesome!" he continued. "Jailbreak, your ride is here!" Then, he called out, "Bee, get the alien a brownie to add to her lunch for being so kind."

"Who made brownies? Did you?" My Mom's voice came from the kitchen.

"There's some in the pantry in a plastic bag, behind the detergent," said my dad.

"What are we going to do with him, Ariel?"

"Hello, Mama Bear," Ariel said just like Chana would. But it was muffled, so I knew she was hugging my mom.

"Sheena!" My mom called up the stairs. "What's she doing up there?"

"May I go up and get her?" Ariel asked.

"Sure. But be careful, she's been punching people lately."

Again, Ariel laughed. When she got to the top of the stairs, she saw me there but kept going down the hall to my room.

I followed her into my bedroom. "Well, hello to you too, Ariel."

"Here," she said, handing me the star from her bracelet. "Hurry."

"How did you know?" I asked as I pulled the Lumen from beneath my pillows.

Ariel opened the brown leather cover and flipped to the back of the book. "Look at the pages at the back, they're already lifting."

"I see that."

She laid the bracelet on top of the imprint on the page like a key unlocking a door. It sank down just enough to open the back, revealing the hidden book behind the first.

We stood close together as the symbols appeared. "This is moving fast." I pointed. "I don't know that one. Do you?"

Ariel was silent for a moment. She slammed the book shut and pushed it under my pillow. "Let's go, Sheena." And just like that, she hurried out of my room, down the hall and the stairs.

I rushed after her. "Ariel, wait."

She continued out the front door as if I wasn't even with her, or she hadn't come to pick me up.

I shook my head as I put on my coat at the front door. *Classic Ariel. I will never get used to the way she walks away when she's done talking.*

We rode to school in her dad's van in silence. Although Mr. Knight was a gleamer, I didn't want to talk about anything in front of him. As soon as he pulled up to the curb in the student drop-off line, I told him, "We can get out here. Thanks!" I jumped out before he could stop me. "Bye!"

Ariel hopped out too.

As we walked, I asked her. "Ariel, what did you see in the Lumen that I didn't see? And you left your bracelet at my house."

"So you can read it later."

"Ariel…"

I hopped in front of her and walked backward to slow her down. "What did you see?"

"Something happened here a long time ago."

"In Muskegon or at Nelson?"

"Muskegon."

"What happened?" I asked, stepping out of her way. I thought it was safe, but she took off again.

She glanced at me over her shoulder. "The path of gleamers."

"The what?" Then I realized it was the same phrase on the bottom of the old map. "So that's good, right? Gleamers have a path."

"No, it's bad. It's very bad."

I sprinted ahead of her and stopped to face her. "Why is it bad?"

Ariel almost bumped into me, stopping just in time. "Don't worry, Sheena. I'm coming home with you after school. I already asked my father."

"But I have to go to detention."

"We'll work it out," she said and walked around me.

I guess that settled it, the conversation was over. We hurried inside the school.

Chana's voice floated down the hall. "Sheena!"

"Hey, Chana!"

As if on cue, Ariel did our bestie gesture with us, and all I could do was laugh. Chana didn't even argue about it for once.

"Hey, double trouble," Teddy said, as I hung my coat in my locker.

"Put mine in there too," said Chana.

"Seriously?"

I pushed the white puffer coat in the top, and Ariel pushed the bottom as Chana shoved the door closed.

"I don't know why we don't check to see if we can get our lockers side by side," she said.

"This late in the school year?" I paused, seeing Bradly coming towards us. She had crazy-huge lashes glued on her eyelids. "Oh my gosh, Chana, do not turn around."

She did the exact opposite.

"Don't say anything."

She didn't have to.

"Bradly, did your parents see you before you left the house?" Teddy asked with a laugh. "Does your mom know you're wearing her lashes? They look like spider legs trying to reach out and touch me."

"Whatever. I look good," said Bradly, batting the super long lashes.

"Who told you that? Chana, do you see your girl?" asked Teddy.

Chana tapped over her phone without looking up. "That's crazy."

"No, look at her."

"That's crazy."

Teddy nodded. "It does look crazy."

"No, you've got it all wrong. That means she's not paying attention," I told him. "Hey, Chana, look! A rat ran between your feet."

"That's crazy."

Teddy snapped his fingers in front of her face.

She pushed him away. "Move. Stop it, Big Head."

I tried not to look at Bradly. My mind said, "Must. Touch. The. Lashes." But I clasped my hands tight in front of me to keep from doing it. Plus, if I looked at her for too long, I would've laughed. My mom would say she looked fast. To me, she looked strange. Actually, she'd done a good job putting them on, and she did have that teen influencer vibe about her. I started to mention that, but she made an announcement.

"I've got something to tell you guys, and I need you to take it seriously."

I braced myself. I thought she was going to say she thought she saw the Murk or something.

She lifted her chin. "I'm in love with Bodhi."

"Nope. Not interested." Teddy walked away. Cameron came down the hall and steered him back to our group.

"What?" I asked in a high-pitched voice, pretending to be surprised. Was this what the lashes were for, since nothing else had worked for her to get Bodhi's attention?

"Really? Who would've guessed," Chana said sarcastically. "Good luck with that."

"You're only thirteen," I told Bradly. "You've been a teenager for like five minutes. You don't know what real love is yet."

"Thanks, Mom." Bradly rolled her eyes. "But one day, after we go to college, we're going to get married," she said dreamily.

"What is she talking about?" asked Cameron.

"Don't get caught up in that. Look, this is what we need to do," said Teddy.

"Touch Bradly," Ariel whispered. She pulled my arm, and I pulled away.

"For what? I don't want to touch Bradly," I whispered back.

"Do about what?" I asked Teddy.

"The kids."

"Why are we talking about this right now in front of everybody? We need to get to class."

"Fine. Just ignore me, then," said Teddy.

"Will do," said Chana as we moved away from the lockers.

Ariel continued to pull at me. Bradly walked ahead of Chana, still in dreamland.

"Don't you walk away. Just walk away, then," said Teddy.

I watched the expressions of everyone who noticed Bradly's lashes. I'd bet ten dollars she'd take them off by lunch.

"Wait for me," Teddy called out from behind us.

We walked to homeroom, but Cameron grabbed my sleeve to stop me from going inside.

"Sheena, hold up."

"You're going to be late to homeroom."

"Forget about that," he said. "Why are you ignoring what's happening? You watched the video. They're kids like us. They didn't ask for this. Some dark force is stalking them, making them turn against their families, for its own purposes. Preying on them to manipulate and control them. Those kids need us. We're all waiting on you to give a directive."

"Like a captain?"

"Yeah, like a captain. What are we going to do? We're wasting time."

I tapped the pointer finger of my left hand onto my right palm. "First of all, I'm not wasting time. You don't have to know everything I'm thinking or doing."

"You shouldn't be doing it alone."

I ignored the quote that Cameron obviously repeated from Teddy and tapped my pointer finger on my right hand's middle finger. "Second, you're doing it again. You get too anxious and ready to just haul off without knowing the details or what we're dealing with."

He watched the kids entering the class across the hall. "Why are you bringing up the past?"

I tapped the ring finger of my right hand this time. "And C—"

"You mean third."

I thought for a moment. *What did I say? Yeah, that should have been third.* "Anywho—"

"Everyone is getting tired of waiting."

"Everyone like who?"

"Anyway," he said, cutting his gaze to mine, "we're in limbo. Come on, just give me something."

"All right. Sheesh, Cameron. I've been thinking." I tapped my chin. "What if everything we've been going through is a test?"

"What kind of test?"

"A test to weed out those not ready. A test to take us to the next level or to graduate us. Or to see if we will truly fight for what we believe in."

A kid stopped at the bins near us and threw his container in the regular trash bin.

"Hey, there's a recycle bin there for a reason, you know," I yelled at him.

Cameron raised a brow. "You mean like how you are about recycling."

"Yes." I crossed my arms. "So if it's true—I mean, a test to prove what you believe—tell me, what *do* you believe in?"

He gave me a blank look. "Uh…"

"That's a problem." I turned to walk into the classroom.

"We believe in *you*."

"That's another problem. Believe me, support me, yes." I pointed at the ceiling. "But I'm not who you should believe in. At least in the context I think you're using."

When I looked back, Cameron was still standing there watching me as the bell rang.

22

"Sheena, you're becoming a regular here," said the teacher who stood at the door and welcomed us delinquents to detention.

A boy looked up when he heard my name. I didn't know him, but I'd seen him around. I sat at a desk a few rows behind him.

After the teacher shut the door, she called attendance. "Sheena Meyer?"

"Why are you calling her name when you just spoke to her? You know she's here," the boy beside me said under his breath.

I raised my hand.

She motioned toward my hand. "Phones away, or they become mine. Homework out."

"This sucks," said a girl behind me.

A boy sitting near the door raised his hand. "I don't have any."

"That's interesting, because your teachers sent over your assignments." She went to her desk and checked her computer. "Yes, there you are. I see your homework right here. Should I print a copy for you?"

"Dangit technology!"

Giggles came from around the room. There were about ten of us there.

"Ariel Knight," she called next.

Ariel has detention?

The door flung open and in rushed Ariel. "I'm here," she said. "Ariel Knight."

"What did you do to get in here?" I whispered as she sat at the desk to the right of mine.

"Nothing."

"Nothing?"

The teacher stood from her desk. "Everyone, Ariel here has volunteered—"

"You volunteered for detention? Are you stupid or something?" asked a boy.

"Out of my classroom!" the teacher exclaimed, pointing at the door.

The boy scowled. "What? Why?"

"We don't call students stupid here."

"But I have detention."

"Take it up with Principal Garcia."

The boy stomped out of the room and slammed the door.

The teacher turned to us. "Does anyone else have a comment?"

No one said a word.

"Good. Now, as I was saying, Ariel has volunteered to tutor math for anyone who needs help. Wasn't that thoughtful of her? Now you don't have to ask for my help." She mumbled the last part, but we all heard her. "From this point on, no talking unless you're getting help from Ariel. And Brent, from what I see here, you'll need her."

"I can't believe she just called me out. Where's Principal Vernon? He wouldn't allow me to be treated like this," Brent joked.

"Ha!" I didn't mean to say that aloud.

The teacher glanced at the clock. "I add another fifteen minutes for all conversations not involving homework."

Everyone quieted, and I opened my textbook.

A boy on the other side of me played hockey using a pencil, tiny balls of paper, and a plastic bottle cap. One of the balls flew over at me, and I tossed it back on his desk.

Ariel leaned toward me. "Need help with your math, Sheena?"

"No, I've got it."

"I can help you," she said again, winking both eyes.

She scooted her desk closer to mine and placed a piece of notebook paper on it with a math problem she'd already worked out. Her flowery scent masked the stale odor of the room.

"That boy keeps staring at us," I whispered to her.

Ariel glanced at him as he watched us over his shoulder. I glared at him and pointed my finger at my desk and made a circle while mouthing, *turn around.*

"Do you actually have math homework?" Ariel whispered.

"I, uh . . ." I watched the boy. He looked to be texting someone under his desk. "I already did it. In class."

The teacher's sharp voice grabbed my attention. "Why are you using your phone?"

The boy stuffed his cell in his pocket, but she wasn't talking to him.

"We need the calculator," said Ariel. She held the phone up, showing her.

"I guess that's okay," the teacher said. She went back to whatever she was looking at on her computer.

Ariel turned over the math sheet. She'd drawn symbols on the back. "I remembered these from earlier. This word is in Latin. I was going to look it up on my phone, but she keeps watching us."

"I'll do it," I said, taking her phone.

Brent raised his hand. "I need Ariel's help."

Ariel went over to his desk and instructed him on his algebra. I never knew she was so good with math. She *did* say her mind worked differently. That's why the Murk didn't understand her, because she's autistic. It turns out, her giddy-self is some kind of math genius.

I looked away and across the room just as the boy with the phone snapped a picture of me.

"Hey!"

"What's wrong?" asked the teacher.

"He took my picture without my permission."

"Who?"

I pointed at him. "The paparazzi in the black jacket. He used his phone."

She lifted her palm. "Phone."

His eyes widened. "I wasn't trying to—I was just—"

"Save it. Hand it over," she barked.

He gave it to her and shot me a mean look. Like that was supposed to scare me? Hmph. He had no idea how low he was on my scale of scary things.

As soon as the teacher announced we could leave, we all snatched up our backpacks and crowded at the door.

"I'm so happy to be out of there," I was telling Ariel when Teddy walked out of the classroom next door.

"There's Theodore," said Ariel.

"Why are you still here?" I asked him.

He fell into step beside us. "Tutoring. I just got out."

"Let me guess, Spanish?" I asked.

"Yup."

"Did it help? Tell me what you learned."

He shook his head. "Nope."

"I promise not to laugh. For real."

He thought for a moment and cleared his throat. "Yo soy Suizo."

"Swiss?" I laughed. "Why are you saying you speak Swiss?"

"I don't know. It's what I remember."

"Qué interesante," I replied.

He cocked his head. "What did you say?"

"Keep going to your tutor."

"That's not what you said."

"Yes, it *werz*—" I was trying to say was but at that moment, a boy shoved me into Ariel.

"Watch where you're going," he snarled.

"Excuse you!" I exclaimed. With a whole hallway to the left of us, he chose to walk between us just to bother me. "That's the kid who took a picture of me in class."

"For what?" asked Teddy.

"I don't know."

"Do you know him?"

"Nope."

"Hey," he called out to the boy, who now had his back to us.

The boy stopped.

"No, Teddy." I tugged his arm. "Don't."

"Shh!" he told me, then jabbed his finger at the boy. "You need to delete that photo."

"What photo?" The boy smirked.

"The one you took of her."

"I can take a picture of whatever I want."

"He called me a 'what'," I told Ariel. "That's insulting."

"Not minors." Teddy told him and pulled a shoestring from below his shirt. He blew the whistle that hung from the end.

Ariel and I looked at each other and then down the hall, hearing three other whistles sound. Footsteps bounded the hallway, and Cameron, Justin, and Bodhi came running from different directions.

"What happened? Are you okay?" asked Cameron, looking from me to Teddy.

"What's with the whistles?" I asked.

"Security. What's up with Paul?"

Cameron knew everyone.

"He took a picture of Sheena," Teddy said, glaring at Paul.

"Why?" Bodhi asked him.

Paul sneered back at him. "I didn't."

"Liar," said Teddy.

Cameron held his hand out. "Let me see your phone."

Before Paul could respond, Justin grabbed him and forced him around the corner to the end of the hall as if Paul was a football blocking sled. I wasn't even sure if the boy's feet were touching the ground.

"Watch our backs," Cameron told Bodhi.

"I'm on it." He widened his stance, looking up and down the hall.

The rest of us rushed around the corner to see Paul with his back against the wall and Justin standing in his face.

"Check his pockets," said Cameron.

Paul held up his hands. "It's too late. I already sent it."

"To who?" Justin demanded.

He didn't respond.

Cameron frowned. "Take his shoes and socks off."

I pulled at Justin's jacket. "This isn't right. Let him go."

"As soon as he tells us who he sent your picture to."

Cameron and Teddy wrestled Paul's shoes and socks off, while the boy squirmed to get out of Justin's clutch.

"Your feet stink, dude. Take these," said Cameron, holding the items out to Ariel.

Ariel shook her head. "I don't want to."

Cameron opened the exit door and threw them outside. "You're walking home barefoot in the snow. Actually, he doesn't need pants either."

"Sheena, get some water to pour on his feet," Justin said. "Let's make sure they ice over good."

"What's wrong with you? We don't do stuff like that." These were not the teammates I knew. Trying to protect me did not give them license to be bullies. "This is wrong." I looked Cameron in the eye. "I don't even know you right now. This isn't who you are anymore."

He looked down at Paul's feet, and then up at the boy's face.

Paul was tough. At least he tried to act like it. But that pants part had him rattled. I could see it.

"Hurry," said Bodhi from up the hall.

"Sheena..." Ariel said. She closed her fist. I turned to Paul and grabbed his hand. In seconds, his body relaxed. I wasn't sure what would happen, but a door didn't open behind his eyes. The best I could determine was that it's not always what I want that will happen, it's what needs to happen.

So what did happen? I put that Ariel super touch on him. Reminding me that I have each type of gleamer gift inside me. If only I knew how to access them.

"You're not what they say you are, are you?" Paul asked me.

"What do they say I am?"

"The enemy."

"Who says that?" I demanded.

"It doesn't matter."

"Yeah, it does," said Teddy. "Let him go."

Justin released him.

"Get his shoes," I told Justin, but I didn't take my eyes off Paul.

Paul gazed at me. "He's lying to us about you."

"Phoenix," I said.

He nodded.

I let go of Paul's hand. "Paul's not a bad person. He's been misled. Apologize."

"I'm sorry," said Paul.

"No, I mean you guys," I told Teddy, Cameron, and Justin. "Or I'll never speak to any of you again."

"But—Sheena..." Cameron stared at the floor.

I waited.

"Sorry," Justin, Cameron, and Teddy muttered.

"I'm sorry," said Ariel.

"Ariel—I didn't mean—Never mind. Let's go."

"What's on your mind, sweetie," Nana asked that afternoon while Ariel and I sat in the family room, eating dessert Nana brought us from the kitchen. I guess she noticed I hadn't said a thing since we got home. Not even to Ariel.

Everything was on my mind. I was back in the trenches. I heard that in a movie and figured I had the definition correct. The gleamer life was a life of persecution. But why did it have to be that way for a kid? This was adult trouble, not kid trouble or newly teen trouble, and not something a slice of lemon velvet cake would solve.

I set my cake on the side table. "Nana, things are getting so weird right now."

"Weird how?"

"There's my friends and there's..." I swallowed. "Nana, the Murk is back. It's different, but it's back—and growing."

Ariel nodded as she watched us from her seat across the sofa.

"Yes, I know," said Nana.

"You do? Then what—"

"Calm down. You're allowing yourself to get worked up." Nana took a bite of her cake and swallowed. "You have control over that. Remember, Sheena. Your emotions get you in trouble every time."

"But what am I supposed to do?"

"You don't have to tell an apple tree to bear fruit. A seed is planted in an environment conducive for growth. Everything it needs is in there. Then it produces an apple. If you'd left it on a counter, it would forever be a seed. But it does what it was created to do, once placed in an environment with everything it needs."

"So you're saying some seed has been planted in me, and I have all I need for growth."

She nodded.

"You're saying the answer is—"

"You can't always rush the answer. Give it some thought. This internal work is vital to your transformation," Nana said. She got up and walked toward the kitchen.

"What transformation?" I asked.

"Into the gleamer you're meant to become."

I sat staring at the television with the remote in my hand, but I didn't switch it on.

The dove that the angel transferred from Mr. Tobias to me. Is that the seed?

With that thought, I picked up my cake and Ariel's and placed them back on the tray Nana had brought them over to us on.

"Water or milk?" asked Nana over her shoulder.

"Both."

Nana came back with our drinks and set them on the tray next to our cake. I stood, kissed her on the cheek and carefully picked up my tray. Ariel did the same, which made Nana giggle. Then, we walked down to the basement, trying not to spill anything.

Ariel followed me and sat on the sofa.

"Thank you," she said as I placed her cake in front of her on the ottoman.

As delicious as Nana's cakes were, Ariel's mind wasn't on her slice either. She focused on deciphering the symbols in the Lumen.

"Ariel, what types of gleamers are there?" I asked as I sat next to her.

She rattled them off quickly as if I bothered her by asking at that moment. "Protectors, healers, Seers, Keens…"

"Keens?"

"They're sleuths. They can figure out anything. There are travelers…"

"Auntie Aria."

Ariel glanced at me, and then at the Lumen in her lap again. "Warriors and guides. There's more too."

I stood and walked around the sofa, thinking about my Drake dream. And then, I remembered something.

"When I was at the skating rink, it was Justin, Chana, Teddy, Teila, and Cameron who were with me," I told her. "They could see Drake and the twins. I thought Drake allowed them to see—like revealing himself. But it was because they have a bit of the gleam inside them, right?"

"No, Sheena. I mean they do, but it's you. They wouldn't have seen him without you." She looked at me. "And another thing... You still act like you have no power, but you do. You glow like a light bulb. You should act like it. The Murk has no power, but it acts like it."

"But the Murk is growing."

"It needs power. It's taking power from somewhere."

"From us," I said aloud, not realizing it. "Ariel, you are so smart. I don't know what I would do without you."

"I don't know either," she replied with a giggle.

I understood now. Chana, being a guardian angel, was super powerful. Her energy alone would've made the Murk fully operational again. But with us, mere humans, it would need hundreds, maybe thousands of us to grow again.

Okay, now that I knew what it was after, where did I come in? How was I supposed to defeat it?

"There are battles taking place in the spiritual realm that we can't see."

I sat back down next to Ariel, watching her finger slide over the page of the Lumen. "That's what my dream was showing me, I think."

Ariel glanced at me. "You dreamed it?"

"Yes."

"Well, things that are happening here are types and shadows of what's happening in the spiritual realm. That's what this says."

"So we're fighting, just like the angels?" I slumped on the sofa with my head back and my hand over my forehead. What I saw in my dream was intense. I got knocked out!

23

By the time Ariel left, I felt a bit lighter. I had some answers. Not to all of my questions, but I was feeling better about those I did have.

With a touch, I changed Paul's heart. My superhero fantasy brain kicked in and imagined me passing on that power to him. And him going around touching everyone, including Phoenix, and them touching others, until everyone's hearts changed. Why couldn't it be that easy?

Now, I sat next to my mom in our family room. "Mom, I was thinking…"

"Yes," she replied.

"If you could have any superpower, what would it be?"

She was preoccupied, reading something on her phone. A frown formed on her face. "Sheena, I can't do that with you right now." She got up and walked into the next room.

I followed her. "What's wrong?"

She spun around. Her eyes darted around the room. Her mouth opened, closed, and then opened again. "It's Logan. He's gone."

"Gone? What do you mean, gone? As in, disappeared into thin air, ascended into the clouds? Spontaneously combusted? What?"

"He ran away."

"See, I told you. He should've stayed here. I never should have let him leave. This is all my fault."

"Now you stop right there," she said, grabbing my shoulders before I could storm away. "You have no control over what other people do. Only over what *you* do. Everything we do is a choice. Our own choice. Understand?"

I nodded, holding back tears and everything I wanted to say in debate.

Where could he be? Could he make it back to us? No. There was no way he could make it from Ohio to Michigan. It's not like he could walk or ride a bike all those miles. I imagined him pedaling as fast as he could down a dark lonely highway with snow and sleet pelting him while yelling, "I'm coming, Sheena!"

A week passed with no sign of Logan. With each day, I worried more and felt like more of a failure because I wasn't doing what I'd promised Luke I'd do.

There were constant calls from Teddy and Cameron, but I had nothing to say.

There were no visitations from the shimmer or anything resembling the Murk. And I didn't ask any questions about the map, the symbols of the Lumen, or anything else gleamer related. It's not that I didn't want anything to do with it. I just needed a break—a vacation from being me. Bye. See ya. Sheena Meyer, Gleamer, is in Hawaii. Aloha.

"Mom, can you check your email?" I asked one evening as we watched a movie. "You need to sign my permission slip. We're going on a field trip."

"Where?"

"We have to sing at a museum downtown."

She raised a brow. "I thought you didn't like singing for an audience."

"I didn't like singing at all the nursing homes."

"Can kids on detention participate in off campus activities?"

I shrugged. "I don't know, but I won't tell if you won't."

"You know what? It will help keep you busy, so it's a definite yes from me."

Two days later, my choir class and those from two others boarded a school bus that took us downtown to a museum. Muskegon always looked different from a school bus window. Foreign, new, and exciting. Just like it looked on the front of postcards. You would've thought we'd never gone anywhere, the way we looked around at everything.

"All right, ladies and gentlemen," said Mrs. Patrick. "You already know. I will only accept your best behavior. We want to be invited back. We're going to exit the bus and walk inside single file. Be quiet and do not touch anything. Once inside, we will form two lines and they will lead us to the area where we'll perform."

"Is your piano here?" a boy asked.

"No, you'll be a cappella. Don't worry, you're ready. Let's go." She climbed off the bus.

"Let's go, Ariel," I said. We waited until the aisle was clear to stand and followed the rest of the choir toward the bus door.

The frigid air almost knocked me back against the steps of the bus. Since we were in single file, I had to stand there in the cold until the line moved. *It's only five steps. Come on people. Move.*

We shuffled into the museum and dropped off our coats in a room I believe was someone's office and piled them on top of each other, forming a mound.

"Shh," Mrs. Patrick said as we filled the hall.

"Line up," we each told the person behind us, then walked to another open area with white shiny tile floors and light pouring in from the large windows.

Jasmine stood beside me, looking distraught. "I think I gotta go."

"Hold it until afterward," I whispered.

"I can't."

"Don't pee on yourself," said Ariel.

Inside the next room, Mrs. Patrick said, "Wait," and put a finger to her lips.

Some of us quieted, others whispered. It was a bunch of nervous chatter. I was even shaking a little.

"I need to warm up my vocal cords. The cold air isn't good for them. Maybe I should scream," said a girl.

"You're trying to get us kicked out, right?" asked another.

"Mrs. Patrick will be so embarrassed. They'll never invite us back here again."

We were cracking up.

"This way," said Mrs. Patrick from the doorway that led to the stage.

She stood straighter than I'd ever seen her with her short pixie cut and tiny hoop earrings. The bridge of her nose and her cheeks were pink from blush. And she wore red and black like we did. Some kids wore white also. It was allowed.

We walked onto the stage and lined up in our rows. Three rows of sopranos stood on one side, altos on the other end, and tenors in the center. We didn't have any baritones.

I looked toward the altos, wondering if anyone else felt a little bit of stage fright seeing the audience so close to us. Usually at these concerts, people rarely smiled at us.

Mrs. Patrick raised her hands to head height and at an angle toward us. Her eyes said, 'watch me', and she lifted her chin slightly which said, 'here we go'. *One, two, three*, she mouthed.

We began singing softly, "Ezekiel saw the wheel..."

Mrs. Patrick gave us her stern "Sing!" face, and we sang louder, "Way in the middle of the air."

When I focused all of my attention on her instead of what was happening around me, I did well. I wasn't afraid at all. It was like the people weren't even there. Hmm... There was a lesson in that.

The audience applauded and we sang four more songs. We got a standing ovation when we sang *Rise Up*. During the last applause, Mrs. Patrick held her arm out to the right, and we exited that way.

We were on a high as we walked out.

"You all sang beautifully," she said in the other room, giving us one of her rare smiles. I was pretty proud of us.

"Stay right here, we're supposed to have a tour before we leave," she told us.

"Cool!"

Our performance was over, so everyone forgot how quiet we were supposed to be. A parent volunteer hushed a few of us.

"You smell like corn chips," a boy said to his friend beside him.

His friend snorted. "Your mama smells like corn chips."

"Stop that. There will be no mama jokes here today," said the volunteer.

"*Your* mama smells like hot dog water," the first boy whispered.

Someone hissed at me. "Psst… Sheena."

Hot dog water? I scrunched my nose, imagining the scent and laughed. I heard my name again and looked to see who was calling me.

Jasmine waved me over to the entrance of another hall.

"Hey, did you sing with us? I don't remember you being in there."

She shook her head. "I was looking for the bathroom."

I pointed at the sign in the hall in the opposite direction.

"I know, but this place is so interesting. I got to looking at things, and…"

"And what?"

She grasped my hand pulled me along. "Just come with me."

We went through a doorway, down some stairs, ducked under yellow tape across and entrance, and entered an area filled with artifacts.

"Why were you all the way back here?" I asked her. "This area looks private."

"I told you, looking. Artifacts and history are my thing."

"Mine too, but this is trespassing."

"I did have to dodge a couple of the staff members." Jasmine bit her lip. "But this guy saw me and told me about some ancient-looking books. I was looking around and found this door. Then, I noticed something from Stephen

Woodruff's novel. Remember the author who came to the school?"

"Yeah." How could I not? He almost got blown to bits at Nana's house.

"This area looks the same as he described below the castle in chapter twenty-three. Word for word. I should know. I've read the series four times."

We were in a long room with desks pushed together on either side and four tables together in the center. Files and books filled the shelves above the desks.

I pulled away from Jasmine as she approached another door. "Where does that lead?"

"To the basement," she said.

"Are you kidding? I'm not going down there."

"Sheena, trust me, you want to see what's down here. Don't be so scared."

This girl is nuts, I thought.

Suddenly, footsteps sounded from the stairs.

Jasmine grabbed my arm. "Duck!"

We crawled under a table, and I tried not to breathe as a man's black shoes walk by. Once the clacking of his heels faded away, we crawled out again and got to our feet.

"Hurry," Jasmine said.

"Isn't it dark down there?" I asked like there was nothing to it, as if I went into random dark basements all the time for fun.

"No, there are lights."

We hurried to the basement door. Jasmine opened it went down first. "Sheena, come on."

Man up, Sheena. You can't show signs of fear. Remember, you're a, gulp, warrior. I looked behind me and then slid my hand over the textured cement wall as I carefully walked down the steps.

When we got to the bottom of the stairs, Jasmine flicked on the light. We stood in a large room full of display tables, boxes, and racks of old paintings and frames. A couple of doors leaned against a wall next to a futon It looked safe enough. A storage area. Maybe I'd overreacted.

"Come on. We're not there yet," said Jasmine.

"We're not?" I followed her, admiring cherubim carvings that flanked a passage on the other side of the room. Angel wings surrounded their faces. She didn't give me a chance to examine them as she led me to the end of the hall. There was no door, just a huge painting of angels across the wall.

"That's weird, why have a hallway if it doesn't lead to anything?" I asked. "Just to show off a faded mural of... I stepped closer. This is really old. What are those—behind the angel wings?"

Jasmine didn't respond. She stood beside me and pointed. "You don't see it?"

"See what?"

"I didn't either at first. But it's just like Stephen Woodruff's book..." She stooped down, pushed open a half-moon shaped hatch on the wall, and crawled inside.

This is a joke, right? Who crawls into a random hole in the wall?

The opening blended right into the mural. It was part of a feathered wing.

"Jasmine?" I called.

"Come on."

I hesitated a moment.

Her head shot back through the opening, and I fell backward into the opposite wall. "Don't scare me like that!"

"Are you coming?"

I stooped and crawled inside after her. "How did you figure this out?"

"It's in Stephen Woodruff's book. I just told you. I thought you read it."

"Oh, yeah. I forgot," I lied. I hadn't read the whole series like she had. Now I wanted to, to see what else he revealed.

We stood, and I brushed off my black slacks. "It's so damp down here," I said, looking around at the stone walls.

Jasmine walked slowly. Past her, the corridor seemed to go on forever.

"I know it's around here," she said. "I was just down here. Oh, there it is. Look."

She turned to me, and I stepped closer to the drawing on the wall she pointed at. Familiar symbols were scrawled across it, and my breath caught.

"What in the entire universe? We need to get everyone here."

"That was my first thought when I saw it," she replied. "I'll get Ariel and Teila. I already texted Cameron. School's out by now, so he should've received it."

I shook my head. "Mrs. Patrick is going to look for us."

"No, she won't. Our parents are coming to pick us up, remember? She'll think we've already gone."

I scuffed the toe of my shoe on the floor, feeling unsure. "Yeah, but we're supposed to be taking a tour right now."

"Okay, if I see her, I'll say you're in the bathroom or something."

Jasmine hurried away. The light from her phone swung back and forth as she ran and crawled back through the hole.

As soon as she was out of sight, I wondered what I was thinking. I was alone in a hidden passage. *What if they locked me in?* I thought. At the same time, it was kind of exciting, like an archaeological find.

Pieces of rotted wood dropped to the floor from the ceiling. I picked one up and crumbled it in my hand.

"Hello?" I said and listened for my echo from the corridor.

There was none, so I did it myself. "Hello, hello, hello," I said, my voice softer each time. I chuckled, and then quieted.

Did I hear someone respond?

24

"Hello," I repeated. My heart pounded as I waited.

There was no response this time.

"I'm imagining things," I said as I fought against panic. "Not today. You're not going to catch your girl slipping. Un-unh, no fear and doubt in this vessel." I bounced around like a boxer as I spoke, and then looked over the wall again.

"What are you trying to tell me? I dub thee Wall of Insight. You want me to know something, don't you? This was put here for me, the last gleamer, the last type-one. I bet you didn't expect me to be thirteen though, did ya?"

I didn't know why I was talking to a wall, but it helped me ignore the trembling growing inside me from being left alone in a secret corridor that adjoined a museum basement.

The path of gleamers was what I deciphered from the symbols. The same words Ariel had read from the Lumen, and they were also the words on the bottom of Nana's map.

It made sense now. The lines below the city on those prints were this place.

"This was the path of gleamers. Where does it lead?"

"What did you say?" Jasmine asked as she crawled through the wall. Ariel and Teila followed her.

"Sheena?" said Jasmine.

I turned away from them and pointed down the corridor. "There's a breeze coming from down there."

We waited, listening to the sound of water running down a pipe.

"I don't see anything," said Teila. "You are way braver than me. I can't believe you waited down here by yourself."

Me either. "Are the others coming?" I asked.

"Yeah, but I better go up and bring them down too." Jasmine took off back to the entrance.

"Hey, say they're part of the choir," Teila called after her.

"She's not talking about everyone, right?" I asked. "That's too big of a group."

"She didn't tell us. I hope not. How in the world did she find this?" asked Teila. "That's so weird."

"I said the same thing. Ariel, look. Check this out." I gestured to the symbols. "How do you interpret it?"

Ariel began to skip toward me.

I held up my hand. "No skipping, Ariel. Do not skip over."

She immediately stopped and walked up to me. She studied the symbols for a moment. "Angelus Bellator."

There are those words again—what Logan called me.

"Angel Warrior," said Ariel. "I looked it up."

"Sounds like a movie title," said Teila. "A movie created from a graphic novel." She glanced at me.

"No, he didn't!" I exclaimed. "Did Cameron finish his comic? Is it about me?"

"You'll have to ask *him* about that, Angel Girl. Isn't that what he calls you?" she said and chuckled. "Cameron and Sheena sitting in a tree. K-I-S-S-I—"

Heat rushed up around my collar. "Stop it. I can't think when you're joking." I think the corridor was too dimly lit for them to see how red I turned. But I could feel it.

"Sorry. You're right. So why does it say, Angel Warrior?"

Logan had said I wasn't acting like the "Angel Warrior"? How am I supposed to know how an angel warrior acts? Where did that title come from? Sheesh, the last type-one gleamer is enough.

"It's like the Lumen," said Ariel.

"That book? Who put this here?" asked Teila.

"I don't know," I said and read the symbols aloud, "The day the Murk ascended from the depths of the earth."

Cameron's voice came from the entrance. "Boo!"

Teila nudged me.

"Stop it," I whispered.

He scrambled through the wall and jogged over to us, looking excited. Teddy followed him.

"Do you have to do everything with style?" asked Teila.

"Don't hate. It's not attractive," Cameron joked.

"How did you guys get here so quickly?" I asked.

"Jasmine called before you guys even started singing."

"Where is she?"

"Covering for us. We almost got caught. We've been up there hiding," said Teddy.

Corey strode into the passage, gazing at the walls.

"Hey, Corey," I said.

"Hey. Whoa. This is crazy." He looked back at Justin crawling in through the door.

I looked behind them. A white, faux fur-hooded bubble coat was missing. "Where is Chana?"

"Didn't you call her?" asked Teddy.

"I thought you did," said Cameron.

They turned to Justin.

"Don't look at me." He straightened and joined us. "I don't even like you guys right now. Some teammates. You heard me asking for help. Why didn't you pull me in? Got me crawling through a tiny door like I'm a hobbit or something."

"It smells," said Teddy. "There's rats too." He kicked at a rock on the stone floor.

"What did she find down here?" asked Corey. "Yo, isn't that the symbol from your book?"

"Yeah, Ariel and I—" I turned to her, but she was gone. "Where is she?"

"She was just here," said Teila.

Corey took off down the corridor, and we followed him.

Work lamps that barely gave off enough light were strung every few feet along the ceiling. Although it looked like an old abandoned passage, someone had added the lamps.

"There she is," Corey said and stopped beside her.

Ariel stood in front of another symbol, digging at a groove in it with an ink pen.

"Ask her what she's doing," whispered Teddy.

"You ask her," I replied.

I touched the wall, and he knocked my hand down.

He shook his head. "Don't touch anything."

"This part isn't stone like the rest of the walls. It's smooth," I said, thinking aloud.

"I'll ask her," said Corey. "What's up, Ariel. Why are you doing that?"

Ariel's pen broke. "It says to. Around the star."

"Hold up." Corey took a toenail clipper from his pocket, opened the file part, and dug at the wall.

Justin wrinkled his nose. "Why does he have a toenail clipper?"

The boys giggled.

"I don't like fingernails, if you must know," Corey replied as he scraped harder over the outline. "This is softer than it looks, but it's killing my hands."

"Let me try," said Cameron. "Maybe you can fill us in on what else it says, Ariel?"

Either my eyes were playing tricks on me, or the star sunk into the wall a little.

Cameron stopped moving. Teddy began to speak, but Cameron held his hand up. "Wait."

We were all silent.

Cameron placed his ear against the wall, and then kicked it. The wall hissed and slid back. He kicked it again. The sound of air being released from a pressurized container filled the corridor as it slid back further to reveal a star-shaped doorway.

"How did you know?" I asked.

"Something clicked." Cameron studied the wall around the new entrance. "There must be some kind of old pulley mechanism or something."

"He builds stuff. He would know," said Corey.

"I'm not going in there," said Teila.

"Yes, you are, because we're not leaving you here," I told her. "And hurry up. We have to get back up to the museum before our parents arrive and the museum closes."

We walked inside the dark room, shining our phone flashlights in every direction of the stuffy area. It looked similar to the last corridor, but older, with no lights. In the center was a machine. It had a wooden box as its base and a metal pillar with some type of mechanism at the top. It was almost as tall as me.

"Hey!" Teddy shouted.

The wall began to close behind us.

"Find a way to stop it," I yelled.

Justin pulled at it. He and Corey held on until just before it closed on their fingers.

Corey felt around and banged on it. "We're not going back that way. We'll have to find another way out."

"See, we shouldn't have come in here," said Teila. "We're going to suffocate. Nobody breathe. Save your air."

"Calm down," said Justin.

I heard something, or maybe I felt it—movement around us. "Shh…"

Everyone was quiet and still. I was about to take a step toward where the noise had come from. My curls vibrated, making me stop. Then a breeze blew them away from my face. I shined my phone in front of me and gasped.

I now stood at the edge of a gaping, black hole.

"The floor is gone!" If I would have taken another step, I would've fallen into it.

"What?" Corey said, shining his phone over me. "Yo, wasn't it there a moment ago?"

"Move up! Move up!" Justin yelled behind us.

"What is happening?" asked Teila, as we all crowded in together.

Dust shot up around us.

We coughed and rubbed our eyes before shining our phones at the ground.

The floor on every side receded until the seven of us stood on a slab of stone about five feet wide, holding onto each other. I was pressed against the machine thing.

"Is everyone okay?" asked Corey.

Cameron shined his light down into the chasm. "I can see the bottom," he said. "But I don't know what that stuff is down there."

"What is this, Sheena?" asked Justin.

I wiped the grit from my lips. "You think I know? I've never been here before."

"How are we supposed to get across?" Teila asked.

"We can jump," said Cameron.

"Are you nuts?" asked Teddy. "We can't make that."

"Maybe it's this machine thing. Otherwise, why would it be here?" I turned toward it, and Ariel screamed.

Her foot had slipped from the edge. Three of us reached for her. She grabbed Teddy's hand, but her fingers slipped away.

I watched in horror as Ariel screamed again and plummeted into the chasm.

25

"Ariel." It was barely audible, but I couldn't speak any louder as I choked back a sob. I'd led my friend down into a crypt. It was my fault. I killed my friend.

While I stood unable to move, with my eyes wide, everyone else screamed and yelled for her.

Schwump!

Ariel came flying back up toward us, then she dropped again.

Schwump!

I shined my phone light down into the pit and watched Ariel bounce again. There was a trampoline down there!

"Grab her!" I yelled.

Schwump!

"Ariel, reach over here!" Teila shouted.

On her next bounce, she reached out to the boys, and they grabbed her. She grinned as Corey and Justin set her down. She was covered in dirt.

"It's okay. We've got you. Hang on to me." I told her.

"That was fun," she replied.

"Please. Nobody else moves," said Corey.

"Is that what's all around us down there? Dirt?" asked Teila.

I don't think I want to find out," I said and turned back to the machine. "It's covered in dirt too. I need a cloth."

Teddy stretched his arm over Teila and handed me his hat. "Here, use this."

"Shine your phones this way," said Corey.

I used Teddy's hat to brush off the instrument.

Cameron looked over his shoulder. "Brush off that bottom part too."

The metal was like brass, and it enclosed disks of glass on the side of the pillar.

"Wait, I've seen something like this. It's like parts of a—" I scratched my head. "Those are lenses. I think."

"Is that a mirror?" Cameron asked.

I stuffed Teddy's hat in my pocket and wiggled my fingers in front of me. "Okay, okay, okay…"

"Okay, what?" Teddy asked.

"I'm trying to figure it out." Where was Jasmine when I needed her with that information from Stephen Woodruff's book? Maybe that's why he put it in there, so the last gleamer would find it and know what to do.

A metal arm extended from the body of the pillar toward me. It housed something oval-shaped—what looked like… *An eyepiece. That's what it is!*

"What are you doing?" asked Teddy. "Is she putting her face on that thing?"

"I think I'm supposed to."

"Let me do it," said Cameron.

"No, Sheena has to," said Ariel.

"Like identification?" asked Teila.

"That ancient thing is not an iris scan or face recognition software," said Teddy.

"Yet it's advanced enough to have us trapped here," I replied.

"That's too easy. Anyone could put their eyes on there to prove they're human. If that's what it wants."

"Her eyes aren't like anyone else's," said Ariel.

I said a fast prayer inside my head.

"Amen," Cameron whispered. He'd prayed too.

"Amen," Ariel repeated.

My friends shined their cell phone lights on me. I lowered my head. The metal was cold around my eyes. As I looked into the lens, the ground vibrated.

"It didn't work," said Justin.

The small section of floor beneath us began to shift.

"This thing is tilting. It's going to throw us off!" said Teddy.

"I'm not ready to die," said Teila.

"Hurry, Sheena!"

They clung to each other and to me.

"It's not working." My voice was climbing.

Cameron reached around and pounded on the machine.

"Hey! Are you crazy?" I shouted. "You're going to break it."

"It probably hasn't been used in years. Keep trying."

We struggled to keep our footing as the platform rocked.

"Push her back toward it," said Corey.

I grabbed at the pillar with both hands and pressed my head against the lens again. Colors expanded in the glass. Blues and pinks and yellows. Then, we heard a grinding sound. At the same time, a compartment opened on the back side of the pillar and light shone from it.

"It's working. Look!" said Cameron.

A platform extended to the other side of the room. Something white shimmered above it.

"What is that?" asked Justin.

"It's an angel," said Teila.

I shook my head. "No, it's a dove."

"It's a projection," said Teddy.

"Go, go, go," said Corey.

We hurried across the plank in single file.

The dove turned back to us as if saying, 'come this way'.

"Did you see that?" asked Cameron.

"It's just a projection," said Teddy.

We were all breathing heavily as we finished crossing the plank.

"I hope it's showing us the way out because I'm ready to leave this place," I said as I brushed the at my hair.

"Why did we have to go through that?" asked Teila.

"To keep the wrong people out, I think."

"How did you know it would work?" asked Teddy.

"I figured, gleamers have this light that shines within them," I said. "I hoped I was right that the lens and mirror mechanism could pick it up like a microscope. That's what it reminded me of. A really old giant one."

"This is some real Indiana Jones foolishness," said Justin.

I agreed. "Yeah, let's hope we don't run into any snakes and creepy-crawlies like in those movies. Let's get going. We have to find another way out."

The dove flew over our heads and dissolved into the mural across from us.

"Ariel, look where the dove landed. Can you decipher it?" I asked, pointing over her head.

"How does she know this stuff?" Justin asked.

"She is a woman of many talents," I replied.

"Evidently."

Ariel studied the mural, then suddenly turned to us. "Do you know your family's history?"

"All of us?" asked Teddy.

"Yes."

"I guess," he said.

"Some," Justin replied.

"Why?" asked Teila.

"Your families have lived here for generations." Ariel gazed back at the wall. "Even if they left, they came back, right?"

"How do you know that?" asked Cameron.

I shined the flashlight from my phone over the wall and read the gold symbols. "It was a city of gleamers."

"What was?" asked Teddy.

"Muskegon. A very long time ago."

"That's what he meant," Teddy said under his breath. He didn't think I heard him, but I did. Mr. Tobias told him something about this, and I needed to find out what.

"Did that make it super holy?" asked Teila.

"No," I replied. "They were normal people like you and me."

"You're not normal."

"Ha, not funny. It says they hid here."

"Why did they have to hide?" asked Justin.

"Listen to this." Ariel pointed at another section of symbols. "Dark spiritual forces are trying to choke out the light of the world. But you are children of light. You are those chosen to spread the glory of His presence and power." She paused. "Go forth in the power provided."

"Whoa," said Teddy.

"So what did they do?" asked Cameron.

"They've unlocked a secret that changes everything."

"A secret? How is the Murk connected to this?" asked Corey.

"The Murk hated Muskegon because of the gleamers," I said.

It couldn't defeat us. Chana had said so. That day on the field when we went sledding after school. I remembered what she'd told the Murk. "How many times have you tried to take us down? That old vendetta has to give. After the big fire in Chicago, you moved here. You tried to destroy this city with the fires of 1874, 1891, then again in 1946. It's always the same. You build your army, and then try to destroy everything by conflagration. We're still here. Haven't you learned by now that you cannot win?"

Then, I thought of the people at that restaurant who tried to save me and my mom. They knew about gleamers. They knew *I* was a gleamer.

Ariel rushed to another section of symbols.

"Go, go, go. Follow her," said Corey.

We all ran after her.

She stopped, staring at the script. "There is a hidden world that can be seen with eyes of light," she read.

"That's gleamers, right?" asked Teddy.

Ariel kept reading. "They intertwine. Once hidden is now set free."

There was a zigzag drawing below the symbols.

"Is that lightning?" asked Justin.

"It's some kind of force," I said. "Seeker of Shadows. It called to him. All he wanted was to find this force. To unlock it."

"Who?" asked Corey.

"I don't know."

"But he was a gleamer?"

"Yes," I nodded. "The Seeker of Shadows reads young in mind, strong in spirit. But the darkness overtook him. He thought he was doing the right thing, unleashing it to save the town and the people. He was tricked."

"Yeah, I think we know it's a trickster," said Teddy.

"Who trapped it the first time?" asked Teila.

"Wait, wait, wait," I said with my hands out. "We are the future. Young in mind." They waited while I thought it out aloud. "These weren't adults hiding down here. That's the reason for the trampoline instead of finding spikes and bones or something at the bottom of the pit. They weren't trying to kill anyone. Scare, but not kill. They were kids. Our ancestors. It was the children they were protecting. They were the gleamers. It was a kid who released it. Back there I read, 'They've unlocked a secret that changes everything'." I paused. "That's it!"

"What's it?" asked Teddy.

"Don't you see?" I looked at my friends. "We can trap the Murk again before it regains its full force. That's what it's afraid of. You know, I think it's in a mad rush to build and grow before we figure it all out."

I pointed at the wall. There were tiny figures on the bottom with lines surrounding their heads representing light. "And it's only a kid who can trap it again."

"And we're kids," said Cameron, giving me a fist bump.

"Look at her. She's at the top of her game. She can handle anything," said Corey.

"No, she can't. She's only thirteen," said Teddy.

"So what are we doing?" asked Cameron, excited that I had finally come around to his way of thinking.

"Making sure we're not the lost generation," I said, reading the words right from the wall. "We have to stop it."

"That's what's up," said Corey, nodding.

"That's what I'm saying," said Cameron. "Where has *this* girl been? Can she stay a while?"

"Not funny, but I get it."

"Wow, I'm really never going to be able to sleep again," said Justin. "After all of this, I'm going to need therapy. Or food. I could use a taco truck right about now."

"Really, a whole truck, huh?" said Cameron. "That's disturbing."

"You know what? I'm—Hey, something is down there," said Teddy.

26

We all peered behind us as if we could see through the darkness.

"It's probably just Jasmine," I told my friends.

"That doesn't sound like Jasmine," said Ariel.

"And she would have to know how to get through the wall," said Teddy.

"Ariel, what do you hear?" asked Corey.

Ariel didn't have to respond, because the low shriek grew louder and hot air shot toward us.

"Go!" said Teddy. He grabbed my arm and pulled me with him.

"What is that? A furnace?" asked Justin as we ran.

"Faster, run faster," Teddy yelled.

A heaviness came over me as our steps pounded down the corridor. I shined my light over the stone floor as we ran. *Carvings?* We were running too fast to make them out.

"Wait," said Teila. She stopped, holding her side.

"Hold up. She stopped," said Corey.

I ran back to Teila. "Are you okay?" I shined my phone toward her and noticed the carvings again. *Fish*. Every few feet. *That's how they found their way.*

"Is this the way we came in? Where is the wall we crawled through?" asked Justin.

I shook my head. "No, this isn't it."

"It turns here, should we keep going?" Teddy asked as he shined his phone down the corridor.

"Ariel, come here. What feeling do you get from whatever is wailing back there?" I asked her.

"She can tell that? Is it the Murk?" asked Teila. "It's Jasmine, right?"

A shriek came from behind us.

"It's not Jasmine. And it's coming." I pushed them. "Go!" But I didn't move.

"Come on, Sheena!" said Corey.

"Get them out!" I told him.

"I'm not leaving," said Teddy.

"Oh, yes you are," said Corey, pushing him. "She knows what she's doing."

Teddy tucked his lips in.

"I promise," I told him. "I'm right behind you, keep going."

"Whatever you're about to do, you're not doing it alone. I'm staying."

"Theodore... I promise."

He stopped fighting Corey and backed away with the others. I knew if I called him by his real name instead of Teddy, he'd believe me.

I waited, trying to see what was coming. Shining the light from my phone didn't help. I could face it. I knew I could. But the kid part of my brain wouldn't listen to the warrior part. At the last minute, I turned to run. My foot landed on something slick, and I slipped and fell on my back.

A rush of hot wind sucked the breath from my lungs. I lay there gasping.

Get up, Sheena, I told myself. *Get moving!*

I sat up, fighting what felt like the weight of the earth bearing down on my chest, and turned on all fours with my forehead pressed to the ground. *What is happening to me?*

A light flashed for a moment, and I looked up. Someone emerged from the darkness, running toward me.

I told them to keep going. What are they doing?

Before I could take another stifled breath, Chana was at my side, helping me stand. She laid her hand flat against my chest. Prickles of energy surged through me, and I was able to breathe freely again.

"Go. They are waiting for you."

I didn't question her, because this wasn't the Chana I did my bestie gesture with. This was the Chana that faced the Murk when it dragged me away when we were sledding. She was strong and powerful.

She used what I called an adult-goddess voice again, and it amplified through the corridor. "You are forgetting the rules of the guardians," she said to whatever was coming.

Chana began to glow, her human form fading. And without a word, she charged into the darkness and disappeared. I didn't see what happened, or what had come after us. But I heard an agonized howl, and it didn't come from her.

I turned and ran.

"I see her, she's coming," said Teddy.

I reached a stairwell just before another turn in the tunnel. My friends waited for me at the top.

"Sheena, what happened?" asked Cameron.

"Where are we?" I replied. I wasn't sure how to answer that question yet.

"The Hackley and Hume Historic Site," he said. "The tunnel splits three ways below the museum. It went from the Hackley and Hume Historic Site to the Muskegon Heritage Museum, to the Muskegon Museum of Art, forming a large triangle."

"How do you know that?" I asked.

"My phone traced it out."

"Did you see Chana? Did she send you this way?"

"Why would we see Chana?" He rubbed his head. "We ran until we found stairs."

"We have to get out of here and get back to the museum," said Teila.

We ran through the Hackley and Hume Historic Site, past the strange looks of the visitors there and worker's cries of "Where did you come from" and "What are you doing back there" and the "Stop those kids".

Ariel, Teila, and I ran the three blocks back to the museum wearing Cameron, Teddy, and Justin's coats. The boys had let us wear them and ran with us in just their hoodies and sweaters.

When we arrived at the museum, Jasmine was waiting in the lobby with our coats over her arm. "What took you guys so long? Didn't you get my texts? Everyone is gone. I couldn't get back downstairs. I hoped and prayed you would find your way out." She brushed at my hair and black flakes fell from my curls. "What happened to you?"

"It's a long story," I replied.

We handed the boys their coats, and just as we walked outside, somebody shouted at us.

"Sheena! All of you!"

We all faced the woman with hands on her hips, taut face, and brows low.

Oh, boy. I'm dead. "Hi, Mom. We were just—"

"All of you need a good whooping. Get over here," she said.

They weren't her children, but my friends obeyed and walked over to her.

"I've got them," my mom said into her phone. "Tell Mrs. Patrick they're okay. Uh hmm... They just sauntered out of the building. Okay, bye."

Ariel's dad could've been on the other end of that call. Or Teila's parents. Or worse, my dad. *I'm in so much trouble.*

"They must've looked for us," whispered Teila.

"Duh," said Jasmine.

"Where have you been?" asked my mom.

"We're gonna go," whispered Cameron.

"You guys get in my car," she told them.

"I'm parked over there," said Corey.

Cameron pointed behind him. "And I'm with him."

"Me too," said Teddy.

"Me too," said Justin.

"Go then, everyone else, my car," my mom said.

The boys waved and ran off.

As Teila and Jasmine climbed into the backseat of our SUV, my mom whispered to me. "What happened? What did you see? And what's this dirt on your face," she asked as she took her glove off, licked her finger, and tried to rub it off.

I was in trouble, so I didn't pull away. "How do you know I wasn't just hanging out?"

"That's not your MO." She glanced at Ariel, who stood outside the car wiping the dirt from her jeans. "Ariel, what are you doing? Get your little-self in this car," my mom told her. "Where have you been, in a chimney?"

Ariel flushed. "No, ma'am." She slid into the backseat with the other girls.

My mom turned back to me. "Just tell me later," she whispered.

No one said a word as we drove. I think the shock of it all had set in.

We dropped off Teila and Jasmine first.

I noticed my pocket bulging. Teddy's hat. But there was something else in there. I'd forgotten about the folded print. I opened it and immediately saw what I hadn't seen before.

My mom glanced over at it, but she didn't say anything.

"Ariel, look at this," I said, passing it back to her.

"My dad has this," she replied.

I spun around. "He does?"

"Yep. Do you know what it is?"

"I do now. A map of what we just saw."

Ariel grinned.

I sat back in my seat. Nana, Justin's grandmother, Ariel's father, and no telling who else had copies of the print. Mr. Tobias had probably had one too. They were all a part of this. At least, their ancestors were.

"What is it, Sheena?" asked my mom. "I can see your mind working."

"I—I don't know. I'm trying to put the pieces of a puzzle together."

"What puzzle?" she asked.

"That's what I need to ask Nana."

"No, *we* need to ask Nana. No secrets, remember?"

"And me too?" asked Ariel.

"No, not today, hun. I'm dropping you off at home."

"Okay," Ariel said, as if she didn't have a care in the world. If I didn't know any better, I would've thought she totally forgot about everything that happened that afternoon.

When my mom pulled up to the house, I almost didn't want to get out of the car.

"Straight to the table," she said when we walked inside. She was suggesting I would go up to my room without telling her where I'd disappeared to. She was right. That had been my plan, hoping she'd get engrossed in something on television or on a phone call with one of her realtors or someone from one of her church groups.

I took my coat off and went to the kitchen table.

My mom took a facial wipe from her purse and wiped my face. "Where did this dirt come from? What is all of this stuff in your hair? Let me see what you showed Ariel in the car."

I set the print on the table and rubbed the folds.

She frowned at it. "That's Muskegon, right? Yeah, I see it."

The floor creaked above us, and someone descended the stairs. Nana walked in.

"You're home," she said with a grin. "Glory be. You look like you've been in a fight on a playground. What's going on?"

She glanced over at the table, and the glass she held crashed to the floor.

"Mama!" my mom exclaimed while pushing her back. She often treated Nana like she was a kid like me.

"I'll get the broom," I said and ran to the closet.

"Is that from my wall, Sheena?" asked Nana.

"No, ma'am. I found this one. Justin's grandmother has one, and Ariel's dad has one too."

Nana sat and lifted her feet as my mom brushed the glass from below them.

I traced out a triangle. "Below these buildings are passages where gleamers hid."

My mom shook her head. "No, there isn't."

"Yes, there are. I saw them."

"You've been there? To the path of gleamers?" Nana asked.

I nodded.

Nana covered her forehead, and then her mouth. "That's only part of the story."

"How do you know this?" my mom asked me.

"We read it from the walls in the passages."

"Sheena, are you saying you read it aloud?" asked Nana.

I nodded. "That's how people read to others."

"Sweetie, the Murk can't read the language on those walls. Reading it aloud, you told it what it wanted to know."

"You told it? Was it there?" asked my mom.

I dared not look her in the eye. "I don't know if it was or not."

It wasn't a lie. I only assumed that's what had come after me. And if I told her everything, I'd have to tell how I got away, which meant bringing Chana into it.

"Let me tell you what I know," said my mom. She took the hair clip out of her hair and shook her locks. She pointed at me. "You're either not telling me everything, or you're not telling me the truth." She turned to Nana. "You know exactly what's going on here. So tell me how this print affects my child."

Nana rubbed her lap. "Sheena is in no danger. It's just an old story."

"Enlighten me."

"There was a time when there was a gleamer in every city. But Muskegon was different. It was a city of gleamers. Imagine a time of peace and friendship and—"

"Forget all the fluff. How does this affect us right now?" She tapped the print. "You dropped a glass when you saw it." My mom didn't miss a beat.

Nana sighed. "One of the gleamers set the Murk free."

My mom's eyes widened. "What?"

"He was tricked."

"What does that have to do with Sheena?"

"Nothing. I told you it's an old story. I don't even know where she got the print."

"Then it's just a print of a place that exists," my mom said, looking back and forth at us.

"Yeah," I replied.

"It's just a print," Nana agreed.

"Good," my mom said and stood.

I smiled.

Nana placed her hands on the table. She extended her pointer finger and turned it left and right.

I stopped smiling and tucked my lips in.

She glanced up at the ceiling. I nodded. That was code for 'we'll talk later'.

I spent an hour in the shower trying to wash that tunnel off my skin and out of my hair. After dinner, on the way to my bedroom, Nana came down the hall, grabbed my hand, and took me to her room.

"I have a lot to tell you," she said.

We stopped in her doorway.

My mom sat in the chair beside Nana's bed. "Good. I can't wait to hear it."

27

"Mom?"

She leaned back in the chair and crossed her legs, placing the right UGG slippered foot on her left thigh.

She's sitting like Daddy would sit. This is not good.

"Like I've told you too many times to count, I've been your age already. I know what you're going to do. You and your partner in crime here." She gestured to Nana.

Nana and I walked in with our eyes low, ready for our scolding. My mom waited as Nana sat on the bed with her back to my mom.

"Sheena, you said there are others who have this print. We are not aware of each other's identities or of how many there are," she said.

"Surely, that's not all you were going to say," my mom replied.

"That's where I was going to start, Belinda. It all starts with that print."

"I'm listening..."

"There's someone here to see you," my dad called from the stairs.

"To see who?" Nana asked.

I yelled it. "To see who?"

"All of you."

I was the first one down the stairs and slowed upon entering the living room.

Justin and Ma sat on the sofa. Ariel and Mr. Knight stood off to the right. Cameron stood with them, holding a picture frame.

"Cameron?" I asked.

"I recognized this picture when I saw it on Ma's wall. This is my grandfather's," he said, handing it to me.

"I told you, Sheena. Your team," said Ariel. She walked toward me and nodded her head at an angle.

What is she—? My feet! I'm wearing my footed unicorn pajamas! Thank goodness I was close enough to the foyer to grab my coat off the hook and put it on.

Cameron smirked at me.

"But why are you here?" I asked.

"I told Ma about what happened today," said Justin. "Then I told her everything. I'm sorry, Sheena, but she knew something was up. She said she saw your gleam?" He looked confused about that last part.

"I told my father too," said Ariel.

I wasn't surprised. I figured she had always talked to him about everything.

"Who are you?" asked my mom. "I mean, I know you, Mr. Knight. But who are you beyond that?"

"Descendants of the city of gleamers," he replied.

Ma stood, and she and Mr. Knight each embraced Nana. Each cradled one of Nana's hands as if they were long-lost friends. Then, the three of them glanced at me. From their connection, they were illuminated in a light so bright, I finally understood what Ariel meant when she had jokingly asked me to turn down my shine a little.

"I'm not supposed to know who you are," said Nana. "These prints were the only thing that identified us."

"Are we gleamers?" asked Cameron.

"No, son. You would know by now if you were," Nana said. "It skips generations. But someone in your family was. You are part of a generation who has a specific destiny."

Ariel nodded, but her and Justin's expressions told me they knew more than I did about the city of gleamers. And whatever it was, it wasn't good.

The adults excused themselves to the next room for "coffee".

Of course, I protested. "I think I should be a part of this conversation. You know, the last type-one gleamer?"

"Stay there," my dad said sternly.

I turned back to my friends with my arms folded. "So is there something you guys want to tell me?"

"Umm…" Justin scratched his head. "I've always believed you. I mean, I've seen—well, you know what I've seen. You were there. But now I'm like, this is really happening. Gleamers are real and in my bloodline." His elbows rested on his knees, and he covered his face with his hands.

"I know that's not what you were asking. I just had to say that," he continued. "Ma says history repeats itself and the gleamer descendants have to come together again. She didn't think she'd live to see the day."

"Come together for what?" I asked.

"Exactly what you already know," said Cameron.

"We're supposed to defeat the Murk?"

"Trap it again, I think. Like you said earlier."

My parents didn't tell me anything about the adults' conversation in the kitchen. Although I felt I had a right to know. They didn't like me keeping secrets, but I could tell they were keeping one, and it was big. They'd avoided eye contact with me and only partially answered my questions or didn't answer them at all.

The only thing my dad *did* mention was why he didn't sense I needed him.

I paced the floor, first waiting for Teddy to call me back so I could question him about Mr. Tobias, and then waiting to hear from Chana. My thoughts drifted to Logan. Where could he be? He knew so much, I bet he knew about the city of gleamers too.

Chana hadn't picked up when I called, so I called again.

"Chica!" she exclaimed.

"What's wrong with you! You know I've been calling."

"You know there's this thing called homework, and my mom took my phone until I finished because she's complaining about how much time you and I spend texting and stuff."

"Yeah, okay. But what about what happened this afternoon?"

"What happened?"

"Here we go again. I need you to be serious because I need to tell you about the new developments at my house." I fell back on my bed. "My mom wasn't playing."

"What did I miss? The dishes in the dishwasher are clean," she yelled. "I've gotta go. I have to put the dishes away. Come over tomorrow."

"Wait! You can't hang up until I tell you about the city of gleamers. They were at my house. And why did you show up instead of my dad? He's so upset that he couldn't tell I was in danger. Something's wrong. I can feel it."

"No way! Are you sure about the gleamers?"

I knew she'd ignore the rest of what I said. "Yes. I mean, not all of them."

"Oh my gosh! I'm—I'm coming," she yelled. "My mom is being impatient. So you're coming over tomorrow?"

"Why don't you come to my house? We can invite all the girls. Just the girls."

"Okay, I'll call them and call you back later. You invite the little cherub. It's a party!"

I sat my phone down. How could Chana think of anything party related with all that was going on?

After sitting a moment staring at my bookshelf, I jumped up and went to my desk. Jasmine had said that what we saw in that corridor was in one of Stephen Woodruff's books.

There was only one of his eBooks on my tablet, and even if it took all night, I was determined to read the whole novel. It wasn't like I'd get any sleep that night anyway. I mean after everything that happened, the last thing I wanted to do was close my eyes—in the dark.

At midnight I threw my blanket off my head, set the tablet down, and stared out my window with my mouth open. "Ariel is not going to believe this."

28

The information from Stephen Woodruff's book was too important to call or text Chana and Ariel about. Instead, I anxiously awaited their arrival.

Teila and Bradly arrived together. Then Ariel came. Chana arrived last.

"Come in and sit down," my mom told them.

I dragged my feet. I didn't want to sit with my mom and friends. Juicy bits of gleamer information were close to bursting from me. I wanted to pull my friends away to our meeting. Plus, it gets awkward because my mom tells all my business. Embarrassing stuff from when I was little.

Next, my dad comes in harassing us. It always happens. We have a rule that he's supposed to stay away when a bunch of girls are over. Only because he acts so goofy and like he's down with whatever we're into. *I'm* not even down with what they're into.

That night, for some reason, my dad was in the mood to learn a dance for a TikTok video. I had to admit, it was fun.

Then somehow, he got on the subject of how he met my mom. "Sometimes you know who you want to be with for the rest of your life."

"Daddy, you're getting mushy."

"No. Let him finish," said Teila.

"He's right," said Bradly. She had already informed us that she was upset about Bodhi. "First he was ghosting me," she said. "Then he flat out told me no about dating. Do you know how it feels when you think you've connected with someone only to find out they don't feel the same way?"

Connected? I never saw that. Bradly got on his nerves most of the time. *She's deluded.*

Although Bradly was the most popular eighth grader in the school, Bodhi didn't care, and it drove her nuts.

"I'm the president of the broken hearts club," she said.

My dad gave me his don't-even-think-about-it expression, and I nodded. I knew he didn't play that thirteen-year-old dating stuff.

When we went down to the basement with our food, I had every intention of telling them about Stephen Woodruff's book, but I turned to Bradly. I couldn't hold it in any longer. "Bradly, I'm going to say what no one else here will say. And I don't know why, because a real friend would tell you this."

"Is she talking about me?" Teila asked, sitting on the sofa with a pretzel in her mouth.

Next to her, Ariel shook her head at me, but it was too late to stop what I'd been wanting to say forever. Somebody had to do it. We were in the friend zone now right? It was for her own good.

"You are way too boy crazy."

Bradly's jaw dropped. "I'm not boy crazy. I just like a boy."

"Yes, you are, and you like a lot of boys. Remember what happened at the mall? You're always trying to get their attention."

"Are you calling me out?"

"No, I think she called *me* out," said Teila.

I shrugged. "I'm just saying."

Everyone was silent for a moment, then Teila said, "I don't know what you guys want to do, but there's this movie on Netf—"

"Well, you're a fraud," Bradly said to me, cutting her off.

I looked at her. "Why am I a fraud, Bradly?"

"I don't know why, but I'll tell you how. I don't care if you see angels or goblins. You think you're such a saint, but you're not. You're supposed to care so much about the world, but have you noticed a thing about anyone else other than Chana? Huh? Have you?"

"Leave me out of this," said Chana.

"Are you carrying hate in your heart, Bradly?" I asked.

"Don't mock me . . ."

Don't do it. Don't you say it!

Bradly stood with her hands on her hips. "Boo!"

Now she'd done it. Bradly knew from back in the day that I cringed when I heard someone call someone else that, and I definitely didn't like being called it.

I shot up from my seat and so did the others.

I placed my hands on my hips. "Are you seriously getting up in my face about this? I'm trying to help you."

"No, you're not."

Bradly

"You have too much attitude, and you're vain," I told her.

"What are you, a saint?"

I grabbed at the air above my head and held a fist out at Chana. "Here, hold my halo."

"Don't give it to me," Chana joked.

"Sheena, don't," said Ariel.

I glared at Bradly. "You're a snob."

She scowled back. "Well, you're not even interesting. No one sees you."

"Oh, I'm invisible now?"

"Is someone talking?" She pretended to look around. "I don't hear or see anyone."

I clenched my fists. "No? Well, how about you get your non-seeing-self out of my house."

Chana choked on the pop.

"Get out!" I told her.

Bradly's mouth dropped. She glanced at Teila, and then she stormed up the stairs and slammed the door.

"What is going on with you guys?" asked Teila. "We should be sticking together, not fighting."

"Tell *her* that." I jerked my head toward the staircase.

Teila shook her head and ran up the stairs after Bradly.

I plopped down on the couch.

"Why did you do that?" asked Ariel. "She didn't take it as a friend looking out for her. She took it as you were judging her."

I looked at Chana for support. She and I talked about how the FPS were all the time. But she didn't make eye contact at first.

"She's your friend now. Isn't she?" asked Chana.

"Yeah, but—"

"There's a time and a place. You should have adjusted her crown, not knocked it off."

I looked at Chana in shock, visualizing what she was saying. I figured she got the whole crown thing from a meme or bumper sticker, but it didn't lessen its effect.

"You're telling her how self-centered she is," Chana continued. "We're thirteen. I mean, aren't we all at this age? Well, maybe not Ariel. But maybe there's a reason why Bradly's the way she is—all boy crazy and everything."

Ariel

"People have different ways of hiding pain," said Ariel.

I looked at the floor. "I'm sorry."

"Tell *her* that," Chana replied, using my words.

The three of us looked up at the ceiling, hearing yelling. I ran upstairs. Bradly and Teila were in the foyer putting on their coats. I looked toward the kitchen and spotted a boy in there with my dad.

"Logan?" I asked.

"Watch your tone, young man," my dad had said.

"Why don't you just tell her the truth?" Logan yelled.

"She's too young to find out she has to die!" said my dad.

29

What?

I backed up. *I didn't hear right. Did my dad say I was going to die?*

I stumbled back and onto my bottom and held my stomach. Bradly must've run toward me, because I looked up at her as she grabbed me. At any moment, I could puke my guts out. I heard Bradly's voice. She sounded concerned. But I didn't understand her words or anyone else's.

This wasn't happening. I misunderstood my dad. That's what happened. He didn't mean it. He'd never say his baby girl had to die. But then, why was everyone watching me? This wasn't my family. They couldn't be. These were imposters.

I'm dreaming, that's what it is. That would explain me going off on Bradly like that, I thought and slapped myself.

"Sheena!" my mom exclaimed, rushing to me and grabbing my hand before I could do it again.

"I—I'm trying to wake up."

"See what this is doing to her?" My mom stared at my dad. "Tell her. Tell her everything right now!"

I was a mile away, listening to her tiny voice. My mind was reeling.

"She has to die" echoed in my head. I felt like I was in a crowded room, with hundreds of people pressed in so tightly I could barely breathe. And at the same time, I was screaming at the top of my lungs, but no one could hear me.

I broke free of my mom's grasp. As I turned over, I eyed the front door. Teila and Bradly had left it open. I sprang up and charged down the hall, grabbed my coat from the hook, and ran outside.

My unzipped coat blew behind me as I ran. The only thing on my mind was getting as far away from my house as I could.

The chilly air filled my lungs. Outside, I was free. I didn't have to die. I had to run.

Their voices called my name, but I ignored them. I was halfway to my school when I stopped, breathing heavily. Glancing in every direction. Which way would I go now? Tears filled my eyes, making it hard to see anything in front of me. A low whine escaped from me.

He said I have to die.

I wiped my eyes and looked at my feet, noticing I was still in my slippers.

I could make it to Teddy's house. I'd be safe there. That's what I would do. Anyone's home, as long as it wasn't mine.

Lightning flashed in the sky, illuminating a cloud I wouldn't have noticed because of nightfall. To my surprise, the lighting hit land at the end of the next block.

Ahead of me, powdery snow lifted in the air and became alive, swirling in different directions. It darkened like a storm cloud until it was almost black.

I sucked in air. My chest rose and stayed there.

No! I slowly stepped backward. A human form flickered inside the cloud and then stepped out of it as if coming through a portal.

I gasped. "Noooooooo! It's not true." I rubbed my eyes again.

"Daddy, I need you," I whispered. The ground had opened, and it was about to swallow me up.

The form fully transfigured. Handsome bad boy features, dark skin, and black clothing.

"Now is when you run," Drake's voice whispered.

BUT THERE'S MORE…

Please Leave A Review

Your review means the world to me. I greatly appreciate any kind words. Even one or two sentences go a long way. The number of reviews a book receives greatly improves how well it does on Amazon. Thank you in advance.

The Sheena Meyer story continues. Turn the page to start reading book six, *Secret of Shadow and Light.*

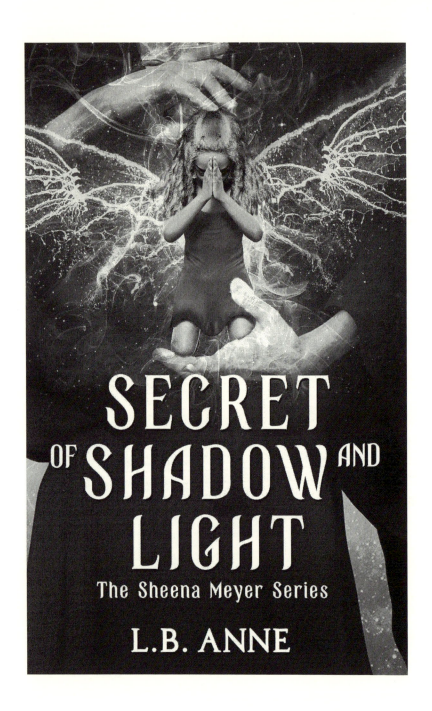

There is a secret that came into being during the age of gleamers. This secret has affected the lives of children all over the world. Contained in its mystery is not only the truth, but a warning. The day will come when that warning determines the course of the gleamer. That day is now...

Giftings have a price.

Thirteen-year-old Sheena Meyer found out the secret attached to being the last gleamer.

All the while, the rise of Phoenix means more trouble for Sheena and her friends.

Now Sheena searches desperately for what will keep her alive. But can she fight her destiny?

Chapter 1

Drake's voice sent a chill through me.

I should've run.

What haunted my dreams and what I thought was in my attic now stared me in the face. If I was still a warrior, I couldn't tell. All I did was stand there. Maybe it was the cold air. It froze my brain or something.

"Let's see what kind of warrior you've become," Drake said as he neared me.

I couldn't believe what I was seeing, but he was right there. The Murk's avatar. The dream had warned me. Why hadn't I understood? My angel had tried to show he was alive, or should I say, rebuilding himself.

Drake stopped in front of me with that wicked grin that would've looked innocent on anyone else. But his eyes told just how evil he was. They bore into me. I couldn't turn away. "We're old friends. Come and say hello," he said. "I'd like to give you a hug."

Did he have control over my feet? They were fighting against me to go to him. I moved like Frankenstein, one foot slightly kicking out and landing on the icy road.

He smirked. "Sheena—"

Before another word left his evil lips, I heard my name in my dad's voice, Logan's voice, Ariel's voice, and Chana's. They weren't coming from a distance, but right behind me.

In an instant, my dad was in front of me, posed like he'd just dropped into the scene and landed like Captain America. Logan and Ariel stood on either side of me.

And Chana... I don't think anyone but me could see her.

"Logan, take Sheena back to the house," my dad said without turning around.

Logan pulled my arm, and I relented, walking backward until I had to turn to keep from falling.

"Wait. My dad may need our help," I told him as I looked over my shoulder.

"No, he doesn't, and neither does your guardian. Hurry," he said.

He could see Chana?

I looked up, hearing a crackling whistle as something came sailing through the sky.

"Let go," I told Logan and broke free from his grasp. He and Ariel fell back from the force that collided with us. But why was I still standing. Then I saw it, the faintest hint of light. Chana. She shielded us as this invisible evil pounded down over us.

"The spirit of a warrior and of a conqueror is inside of you, Sheena, receive it," Luke had told me. But I wasn't being a warrior. Drake terrified me.

A blood-curdling screech came from behind us. In seconds, my dad was there, lifting me into his arms as if I were as light as a loaf of bread. "Come on!" he told Logan and Ariel.

"Everyone, inside!" my dad said as we reached our house.

We raced inside, and Logan slammed the door behind us.

My mom rushed to us. "Jonas, what's happening?"

He didn't answer as he set me down, went back to the door, looked around outside, and then shut it again.

He marched down the hall and pointed at me. "You do not leave this house. Understand?

"Do you understand?" he asked in a harsher tone.

"Yes, sir." There was no doubt about it. I was never leaving again. They'd have to drag me out kicking and screaming.

"Bee, call Logan's uncle and tell him Logan's safe. Girls, come with me," he told Teila, Bradly, and Ariel. "I'll give you a ride home."

Chana suddenly walked into the room.

"Where did you go?" asked Teila. "We thought you were left."

She pointed behind her. "Bathroom."

My dad turned to her. "Grab your coat." He looked back to my mom. "We'll talk when I get back."

Chana glanced over, put her thumb beside her ear and pinky finger by her mouth, before following my dad outside. I nodded.

Teila and Bradly looked concerned but didn't speak. Teila half-waved. Ariel ran over and hugged me. I didn't hug her back.

"It's okay, Sheena," she said. "You can handle anything."

I sniffed and wiped my eyes. "You know what?" I replied. "It's exhausting trying to live up to your expectations of me."

"Sheena!" my mom exclaimed.

Ariel's eyes were still as bright as ever, but her smile faded as she backed away and left out the side door. My mom waited there to lock it as soon as they exited.

I'd never seen the slightest bit of sadness from Ariel, other than on the anniversary of her mom's passing—until now. And I caused it. But at that moment, I didn't care. Why would I care about hurting someone's feelings after hearing I'm going to die and coming face to face with the Murk?

I felt lightheaded and grabbed hold of the sofa. "Sit down," Logan said, guided me, and sat next to me. "Sheena—"

"What are you doing here," I whispered. My voice shook.

He placed a hand on my shoulder. "Are you all right? It's going to be okay."

"It will not be okay. You said it yourself. I'm going to die. I don't understand what's happening in my life." My voice was filled with the tears that were no longer flowing from my eyes.

"'All things work together for—'"

"Scripture. You're quoting scripture? I don't care about that right now. I'm fed up with it. All of it."

I got up and tried to walk away, but my mom stepped in front of me. "Sit down, young lady."

"Why do I have to sit?"

"Because I said so, and don't make me say it again."

You would've thought I was pushed into a chair, the way I plopped back down on the sofa.

Logan sat there as if he were in trouble too.

My mom crossed her arms. "Now, we're going to wait for your father and discuss what you overheard."

"That I'm going to die. Just say it. There's nothing to hide now."

Nana entered the room and sat across from me. She looked tired. Even though she was a grandmother, she didn't have many wrinkles, but there were lines across her forehead. She sighed and stretched her hands across the coffee table to the center.

"Come here," she said.

I hesitated. I didn't want comfort. I wanted to do like people did in the Bible days and tear my shirt and cover myself with ashes. And—and scream and cry until I had no voice and I looked like a prune because I'd cried all the fluids from my body.

But then I noticed the pain in Nana's face, something I'd never seen.

I stretched my arms forward and placed my hands in hers. Nana's hands were soft and warm, and as her thumbs rubbed over my fingers, I looked up at her eyes. A door opened behind them, and I saw it. The whole thing was right there in that journal Nana kept. The prophecy of the last gleamer, but within it, there was a hidden secret. Somehow, I'd missed it when I was snooping that time.

So it was true. The last gleamer had to die.

My mom and Logan watched us and waited. They didn't make a sound.

When Nana released my hands, I backed away and went straight to my room. No one tried to stop me. I don't know if it was my expression or what, but they knew I needed to be alone.

Chapter 2

I turned on my lamp, climbed into bed in my clothes and didn't get out of bed that day or the next, except to use the bathroom. My mom didn't make me either. I drank a little water my mom set next to the bed, but I didn't eat. My hands shook, and I couldn't get warm. At one point, I heard my parents whispering in the hall. My mom said she was worried and wanted me to see a doctor. Yeah, so I could tell them about my gleamer life? That would be just great.

After waking from a nap, I lay staring at the ceiling. There was a knock at my door, but I didn't answer.

It creaked open, and I closed my eyes and breathed long and hard.

"You're not asleep," said Teddy.

I opened my eyes.

"What's going on with you?" he asked. "No one has seen or heard from you. And that Phoenix guy, his whole we-are-the-kids-of-the-future yadda, yadda, yadda movement is growing."

I looked away with my blanket pulled over my face, up to my eyes.

Teddy sat at my desk. "Can you really afford to miss any more days of school this year?"

I rolled over, away from him.

"And why are your parents letting you? Are you sick? Does Chana know you're like this?"

"Probably," I replied, sounding hoarse. "I'm not talking to her either. She should have told me."

"Told you what?"

How do you tell someone you found out you're going to die? And Teddy, of all people. I couldn't find the words. This was Teddy. He was family. It would only hurt him and leave him in the same state I was in. So I did what I had to do for his benefit.

"I have the flu."

He huffed. "No, you don't. This is about that whole you having to die thing, isn't it?"

I sat up. "Who told you?"

"Bradly."

"She should mind her business. I'm going to—"

"You're not going to do anything. She was worried."

"You're not upset about it?"

"Of course not. I don't believe it's true. But you do. *That's* why you're in bed." He shook his head. "Oh, ye of little faith."

"Faith?" I snapped. "My own father said I'm going to die. There's nothing else to say."

"Did he explain?"

"Well, no. Not exactly." I hadn't given anyone the opportunity to say anything else about it.

Teddy lifted the palms of his hands like a scale. "Does that mean yes or no?"

"Knock, knock," Logan said as he knocked on my door. "May I come in?"

I frowned. "Looks as though you already have."

"You got her to talk," he said to Teddy.

"Yeah, I have that way about me. I aggravate her until she wants to scream."

"Whatever works. Is it okay if I interrupt?"

"It's fine with me," said Teddy.

Logan stepped closer to my bed. "I really need to talk to you."

I pulled my blanket over my head. Death was a subject I wasn't ready to discuss. Kids didn't talk about that kind of stuff. "I'm tired. Everyone out."

"But, Sheena," said Logan.

"Out!"

"One day, you're going to have to stop pushing away the people who care about you," said Teddy.

"No one cares!" I yelled at the door as it closed.

Did you enjoy the preview?
Get your copy of *Secret of Shadow and Light.*

Don't miss out!
Exclusive content, discounts and giveaways are available only to L. B. Anne's VIP members. Sign up at lbanne.com. There's no charge or obligation.

ABOUT THE AUTHOR

L. B. Anne is best known for her Christian middle grade, Sheena Meyer, series and doesn't mind being dubbed the "Angel Author." She lives on the Gulf Coast of Florida with her husband and is a full-time author and speaker. When she's not inventing new obstacles for her diverse characters to overcome, you can find her reading, playing bass guitar, running on the beach, or downing a mocha iced coffee at a local cafe while dreaming of being your favorite author.

Visit L. B. at www.lbanne.com/home

Facebook: facebook.com/authorlbanne

Instagram: Instagram.com/authorlbanne

Twitter: twitter.com/authorlbanne

Made in the USA
Monee, IL
06 December 2021